"Nothing's changed," she said.

"Everything's about to change," he argued.

"I'm still who I am."

"I've never asked you to be anything different. You're perfect just the way you are."

Pewter-gray eyes nailed him. "Do you love me?"

Did he? His heart quickened at the same moment his tongue stuck to the roof of his mouth. *Go on. Tell her what she wants to hear.* Trouble was, he didn't much believe in love.

Harlan stared into Lilah's eyes. She was everything a man wanted in a woman. The better question was—what did she see in him? He'd brought her nothing but trouble.

She was also going to be the mother of his child, and he wanted her in his life.

"Time's up. I've got my answer," she said softly, turning away from him.

"Lilah, wait. You know I—" Great. Now he'd found his voice?

She never turned. Her footsteps padded down the hallway, and then came the firm *click* of a closed door.

APPALACHIAN PREY

DEBBIE HERBERT

HARLEQUIN INTRIGUE®

This book is dedicated to Maxine Brooks,
one of the best readers ever!

And, as always, to my husband, Tim; my dad,
J. W. Gainey; and my sons, Byron and Jacob.

ISBN-13: 978-1-335-52617-5

Appalachian Prey

Copyright © 2018 by Debbie Herbert

PLEASE RECYCLE
THIS PRODUCT IS RECYCLABLE

Recycling programs
for this product may
not exist in your area.

This edition published by arrangement with Harlequin Books S.A.

For questions and comments about the quality of this book, please contact us at CustomerService@Harlequin.com.

Printed in U.S.A.

Debbie Herbert writes paranormal romance novels reflecting her belief that love, like magic, casts its own spell of enchantment. She's always been fascinated by magic, romance and gothic stories. Married and living in Alabama, she roots for the Crimson Tide football team. Her eldest son, like many of her characters, has autism. Her youngest son is in the US Army. A past Maggie Award finalist in both young adult and paranormal romance, she's a member of the Georgia Romance Writers of America.

Books by Debbie Herbert

Harlequin Intrigue

Appalachian Prey

Harlequin Nocturne

Bayou Magic

Bayou Shadow Hunter
Bayou Shadow Protector
Bayou Wolf

Dark Seas

Siren's Secret
Siren's Treasure
Siren's Call

Visit the Author Profile page at Harlequin.com.

CAST OF CHARACTERS

Lilah Faye Tedder—As the daughter of a legendary moonshiner, Lilah's used to keeping secrets. But her biggest secret is her pregnancy. When she's forced to return home, she discovers trouble brewing—the kind that could get her killed. As secrets bubble to the surface, she has no choice but to face them...and the man who rejected her.

Harlan Sampson—A deputy sheriff with ambitious plans, he's been warned to stay away from Lilah Tedder. But he can't forget the passionate week they shared, and he's determined to win her love. Trouble is, she wants nothing to do with him. Whatever the professional cost, he intends to marry the mother of his unborn baby and save her from a killer.

Darla—Lilah's elder sister and complete opposite. She steals a portion of their family's estate, and pays dearly for this transgression.

Uncle Thad—The charismatic leader of the family business. Is there a dark side behind his generosity and good nature?

Sheriff J. D. Bentley—Is he an upright law enforcement officer, or is he in league with the criminal element in the county he's sworn to protect?

Uncle Jasper—Reclusive, but with an apparent fondness for his niece Lilah. He knows the family's secret history, but will he help Lilah and Harlan find the killer, or will he stop at nothing to keep the past buried?

Chapter One

Moonshine again...seriously?

Hidden caches had turned up everywhere in her father's cabin. No surprise there. Lilah snatched two plastic jugs from the back utility room and marched to the kitchen, intent on pouring the illegal hooch down the drain. Corn liquor had destroyed her parents' marriage and her dad's liver. Would have killed him, too, if he hadn't been murdered a week ago.

Unexpected tears blurred her vision as she unscrewed the lid on one of the jugs and poured the liquid poison into the chipped enamel sink. Not that she and Dad had been all that close in recent years, but still, the man had been her father. Lilah tipped the jug. *Glug, glug, glug...* a hundred dollars' worth gone. Could have bought a used college textbook with that money.

She blinked and gazed out the open window. The cabin was nestled in the foothills, with rolling mountains standing sentinel in all directions like a green fortress. A deceptive beauty, as though the price for living in such a visual feast meant being taxed with rampant poverty and violence. Dad's death was the latest evidence of that.

Whoever said you can't go home again was dead wrong. After a mere week, Lilah felt like she'd never left Lavender Mountain. Memories washed over her, most of them unpleasant—her parents' screaming matches, brutally cold nights where they'd all huddled in front of the fireplace. But it hadn't been *all* bad. Some days, wandering the woods with her older siblings, Jimmy and Darla, had been magical.

A faint scrape of boots on leaves and pine straw jarred her senses. Someone approached.

Lilah stilled, picturing in her mind's eye the open front door and windows. Had the murderer returned? She fought the instinct to flee to the back bedroom and lock herself in. Probably just one of Dad's old customers who hadn't gotten the word yet.

Quickly, she raced across the rugged pine floorboards to the den. Through the battered screen door emerged the silhouette of a tall bearded man dressed in denim overalls. What mountain had he just climbed down from? Lilah sprinted to the door and latched the rusty lock into place. A joke of a defense. She reached for the weapon always propped by the door frame, and her right hand curled around the barrel of the twelve-gauge shotgun, its metal smooth, familiar and comfortable.

And loaded.

"What you want?" she called out in her fiercest voice.

The man didn't appear the least bit intimidated as he shuffled forward, his foot on the first porch step. "I got bizness with Chauncey Tedder."

"Guess you could say my dad's out of business," she said, sliding the shotgun next to her hip.

He climbed the second step. One more and he would be within six feet of where she stood. He swayed and squinted, peering into the room. Lilah was painfully aware he could see straight into the little kitchenette.

"Looks to me like you got some 'shine in there," he boomed. "Go git me a jug afore I get really riled."

She didn't aim to find out what the stranger was like "really riled." This place was well out of range for anyone to hear if she screamed, and Dad was shot not far from the cabin. Lilah unhitched the lock and kicked open the screen door. She drew the shotgun up to shoulder level, finger twitching at the trigger. "I repeat—this place is closed for business. I'd appreciate you spreading the word."

"Whoa, little missy." He threw up his hands and backed away. "Don't mean ya no harm."

He tripped on the step and took a tumble. *Oomph*.

Chagrined, Lilah bit her lip and lowered the shotgun. "You okay there?"

He rose, brushing dirt off his overalls. "I reckon. You sure are a touchy thing. Best be gettin' on my way." With one last sorrowful glance at the jugs on the kitchen counter, he ambled away, gingerly limping on his right foot.

What the hell.

She returned inside, retrieved the full jug she hadn't yet dumped out, and stepped out onto the porch. "Hey," she yelled. "Come on back, you can have a jug."

He shot her a wary look, clearly suspicious of her change of heart. But in the end, the pull of the moonshine outweighed his reservation, and he returned.

Lilah set the jug down at the bottom of the stairs and scampered back to the door.

"Same price as always?" the man asked, carefully pulling out a wad of dollar bills from his side pocket.

"It's on the house. Just don't come back, ya hear? This is the last of it." Unless she found more while cleaning out the cabin. No telling how many bottles were tucked away in nooks and crannies.

A grin split his weathered face as he tucked the money away. "Thank you kindly, ma'am."

He picked up the jug and gave a quick nod before walking across the yard. A sheriff's cruiser rounded the bend in the road and turned into her dirt driveway. The man momentarily froze at the sight, and then took off running to the nearby tree line—more like hobbling with his injured foot—but almost quick enough to get out of sight. *Couldn't have hurt too bad*, she mused.

The cruiser came to an abrupt halt, and a man started to climb out.

Lilah's heart skittered, even faster than when the stranger had suddenly appeared at her door minutes ago. Could it be…

Oh, yes, it most definitely was.

Harlan Sampson. The man who'd quickly won her heart three months ago and then had dumped her twice as fast after a week of fun and games. Her left hand involuntarily fluttered over her stomach, and Lilah hastily jerked it away.

"Well, looky here," Harlan drawled, eyeing the man carting his haul off into the woods. He faced her and pushed the dark sunshades up on his head, revealing the startling beryl-blue eyes that had enthralled her on her last ill-fated visit, which—*damn it*—still sent her heart pounding into overdrive. He walked toward her. "Looks like I finally caught a Tedder point-blank in the act of distributing illegal whiskey."

"Wrong. I wasn't selling. I was giving. Ain't no money exchanged hands here." Inwardly, Lilah winced at the slip into the local vernacular. It had been twelve years since she'd called Lavender Mountain home, but in times of high emotion—and now definitely counted— she lapsed back into the lingo.

"So you say."

She pinched her lips together. "What brings you here?"

"Came to pay my respects, see how you're getting on."

Weeks ago, she would have flung herself on Harlan at those words. But not now. "I'm jim-dandy," she replied, lifting her chin a fraction. "I saw you at Dad's funeral. No need to come over."

"I believe I owe you an apology."

"Forget it." There was no way she'd admit how much his silence had hurt.

His eyes smoldered, and he slowly climbed the porch steps, close enough now to make her breath hitch. "I can't forget it. And I can't forget you."

EVEN GLARING AT HIM, shotgun by her side, Lilah Faye Tedder was a hell of a sight. Harlan drank it in—the long blond hair that tumbled past her shoulders, the elfin delicate face with the determined chin, the slight womanly curves of her body. He had tried to wipe away the memory of her, but with one glance, the old familiar pull returned. He nodded at the firearm. "Mind putting that thing away? Hard to talk to an angry woman holding a shotgun."

A smile ghosted across her face before the hardened set returned to her chin. "You said what you came to say. Apology accepted."

"C'mon, Lilah. Let's talk."

She hesitated, then shrugged. "Suit yourself."

With that, Lilah spun on her heel and entered the cabin. Not much of an invitation, but he'd hardly expected her to welcome him with open arms. The place smelled as clean and as fresh as the pine breeze that blew through the open windows, but with a touch of lemon cleaner. It already had the stale antiseptic look of a bare shell of a dwelling. No knickknacks or frivolities, just an old sofa and a couple of chairs.

"I see you've been hard at work." He'd been here before. Chauncey's old place had been filled with junk when he was alive.

"It's all set for the realtor to list as soon the reading of the will is over. After that, I'll head on home."

Probably for the best, at least for his career. According to Sheriff J.D. Bentley, associating with any Tedder wouldn't reflect well on him or the office. His boss planned on retiring soon and understood that he had ambitions to run and take over the top law enforcement job in the county. And as such, J.D. had driven home the point that he had no chance of winning the sheriff's election if he was a known associate of the outlaw family.

Personally, Harlan couldn't care less about the piddly amounts of money some moonshiners made. No, what disturbed him were the rumors that Lilah's family had turned to the new Appalachian cash crop of growing marijuana.

Following her lead, he took a seat in one of the old chairs that remained. "No reason to hurry home, is there? Now that school's out, I thought you would be free for the summer."

She leveled him with a glacial stare. "That was the original plan. Things changed."

Ouch. Yeah, he caught her barb. Last time she had been home, they'd planned on her returning to Lavender Mountain this summer so they could see each other regularly.

"Sorry about your dad. Must be hard—"

"Any news on who shot him?" Her voice was sharp and cold.

"Not yet," he admitted. "But we're working on it."

"I bet."

This wasn't the same Lilah from March, the woman with the ready smile, the soft eyes and the gentle voice. But she had every reason to be bitter, especially with him.

"We're working 'round the clock. No leads have panned out yet, but we're interviewing his friends and—" he hesitated a beat "—known associates."

"Meaning y'all suspect this was related to his moonshining."

If only it were that simple. He hedged. "The theory is it revolved around his illegal activities, yes. You and

Darla already said he had no enemies or problems with others that you know of."

Silver eyes clouded in pain. "It makes no sense. Why would anyone shoot Dad? It's not like he made a fortune." Her neck turned a fraction toward the back of the cabin.

"Maybe an irate customer?" he suggested.

"Doubt it. Most were regulars." Again, her eyes darted to the rear of the cabin as she folded her arms at her waist.

"Okay, what's going on?" he asked sharply.

Her eyes widened. "I don't know what you're talking about. Nothing's going on."

He strode past her, down the narrow hallway and peeked inside the two bedrooms at the end. One was completely empty, nothing suspicious there. The other housed only a double bed and a dresser. A lacy pale yellow nightgown was draped across a plaid bedcover. An image of Lilah in that nightgown flashed through his mind, and he gritted his teeth at the wave of loss that churned his gut.

"What do you think you're doing?" She followed close behind him, her bare feet padding on the old wood flooring. "You have no right to search my place."

"It's not yours until you can show me the deed has been transferred to you in writing." He crossed the room and glanced cursorily inside the small bathroom with the old-fashioned iron claw-foot bathtub. Nothing out of place there, either.

"Mind telling me what you're looking for?"

He felt a tad foolish for wondering if an unwelcome visitor might have forced his way in and held her hostage.

"Well?" she demanded.

"I'm not sure. But you kept looking back this way, as if something was worrying you."

A flush stained her cheeks. "You're imagining things."

This was getting him nowhere. He changed tactics. "Lilah, I want to help. If there's a problem, tell me. I can't leave you alone out here if there's the slightest possibility you're in danger."

"Why do you care?" she scoffed. "Go on and leave me—again. It's what you do best."

Her words slammed into him like bullets. He'd hurt her. Bad. "I'm sorry," he said, shuffling his feet. "I should have at least tried to explain."

"No explanation needed. I can guess what happened. As soon as your family and friends caught wind of you seeing a Tedder, they jumped all over you. Go on, admit it."

Heat rushed up the back of his neck. She'd pretty much nailed their reaction. He could have borne their objections, but...

"And then your boss piled on, too. Right? Wouldn't look good for the apparent heir in the upcoming sheriff's election to be sleeping around with a lowlife like me."

The accusation in her eyes stung, but not as much as the truth of her words. Yes, he was ambitious. But it wasn't the money and the power he craved—it was the chance to make a difference. This little corner in the Appalachian foothills had always garnered more than its share of hardship and tumult. And somehow, the situation kept going downhill. Elmore County was rife with drug trafficking, ancient feuds and an isolation that led many to a life of crime, believing the laws didn't apply in this neck of the woods.

"I won't deny any of that," he said slowly. "J.D. had a long talk with me. Basically said that if I continued seeing you, he wouldn't endorse me as his replacement."

"And your career means more to you than I do. Fine. But you could have talked to me instead of giving me the silent treatment."

"You're right. And I regret that."

Harlan regretted a lot of things. He should never have listened to J.D. or anyone else. He should have defended Lilah. He should have never let her slip away.

He was an ass.

Harlan shook his head. No, he'd done the right thing. The people in this county needed him. No point in throwing his career away because of one magical week. But that one week together during her spring break from work and school had been an unbelievable whirlwind of passion and emotion. And then, he'd slipped out of her life without a single word, even after all the plans they'd made for the summer. He raised a hand to touch her, to cup her face in his palms, to tell her he was sorry.

Lilah stepped back, lips curled in a bitter smile. "Don't even think about it, Harlan Sampson. We're done."

Abruptly, he dropped the hand by his side. He'd lost the right to touch Lilah ever again.

"Message received." He took a deep breath and

straightened his spine. "But I still don't like leaving you alone out here. Can't you get a room in town until you've finished your business?"

"No."

She turned and headed down the hallway, leaving him no choice but to follow. Lilah opened the front door wide and waved a hand in dismissal. "Goodbye, Harlan."

He nodded, but as he brushed past Lilah, he couldn't resist placing a hand on her shoulder. "I'm sorry for everything. And for your loss. Your dad might have been on the other side of the law, but he was a decent man. I liked him, and he didn't deserve what happened. I'll do everything I can to find who shot him."

The anger and hostility fled, and her lips trembled the slightest bit. "Thank you," she whispered.

"Is there anything I can do for you?"

She shook her head.

"If you think of something, you have my number."

Before she could object, he planted a light kiss on her cheek and stepped out onto the porch. The sun was sinking low in the green mountains, casting a coral and purple hue on the clouds. Damn, he hated leaving her with night approaching.

"Wait. There *is* one thing you can do."

He swung around, eager to help. "Name it."

Lilah lingered in the doorway, rubbing her arm. "I—I found some money today while I was cleaning up the place. In light of what happened to Dad, well, it makes me nervous. It's too late for me to go to the bank, but maybe you could keep it safe for me tonight? I'll come pick it up in the morning and deposit it."

"No problem."

He returned to the inside of her cabin. How crafty of Chauncey to keep a hidden stash of dough. He hoped for Lilah's sake that it was at least a thousand dollars or so. She could use the cash. Working as a teacher's aide and going to college didn't leave her much in the way of money.

"I told Darla 'bout finding a wad of cash up under the mattress, and she wanted us to go on and split it, but I told her it didn't sit right with me. That much money should be reported."

He gave an indulgent smile. "No one would be the wiser if you didn't turn it in. There's no need to worry. I agree with Darla, just keep the money."

"But it's a lot of money. I'll need to talk to the bank manager. Don't they investigate if you deposit more than ten thousand dollars at a time?"

The *hell*. "Excuse me? How much money are we talking about?"

"About thirty thousand."

Thirty. Thousand. Dollars. Ill-gotten dollars, no doubt. The rumors must be true. Chauncey, and probably his partner-in-crime brother as well, had graduated from moonshine to marijuana—or even harder drugs.

"Get it," he said tightly. Small wonder the Tedder reputation stank.

And she'd planned on sleeping on that load of cash tonight? Some folks 'round these parts would kill for thirty grand. Even if Lilah knew how to use that shotgun, she'd have been putting herself in jeopardy staying here overnight with that much money. If anyone else knew about it, she could have ended up with bullets riddling her body—the same fate as her father.

She scampered away, seemingly eager to be rid of the cash. Hard to believe, but at some level, Lilah must still trust him. Damn, he would have to tell J.D. about this. No way he could just let her waltz into a bank and get flagged as a possible drug dealer.

He sat on the sofa and ran a hand through his hair. "What the hell did you get mixed up in, Chauncey?" he muttered under his breath. He kicked back on the cushions and sighed.

Sure was taking her a long time. Harlan drummed his fingers on the wooden arm of the old couch, waiting.

And waiting.

"Everything all right, Lilah?" he called out.

She staggered back into the den, face pale and fiddling with the gold cross chain around her neck.

He stood, dread prickling his scalp. "What's wrong?"

She drew an unsteady breath. "The money…it's gone."

Chapter Two

Gone.

Harlan rubbed his temples and sat back down on the sofa. He pointed to the rocker, and Lilah settled across from him. How to tell her?

"Was your dad in the habit of keeping large amounts of money around the cabin?" he finally asked.

"No." She clasped her hands in her lap. "At least, not that I'm aware of."

"Any idea how he might have come into this money?"

Her lips pinched together. "No."

"Moonshining can be pretty profitable for a few folks."

The muscles in her jaw worked, and she lifted a hand and waved it in the air. "Not for us. Does this look like a mansion or something? If Dad made much money at it, he sure didn't believe in spreading the wealth."

Harlan knew her financial struggle. She'd been working for six years as a teacher's aide, paying for college tuition and books as she could on her salary.

"Sure, he wasn't known for having an extravagant

lifestyle," Harlan agreed. "But you told me yourself that he acted different when you visited in March."

"Lots of shady characters hanging around. A younger crowd, people I'd never seen before." She sighed and stared down at her hands. "Lots of long talks with Uncle Thad, too. Whenever I entered the room, they would stop talking. But that wasn't so unusual. In the past, they would come up with some pretty harebrained get-rich schemes that never worked. Part of the reason Mom cut out years ago."

Lilah lifted her head and faced him dead on. "But you already know most of this. I confided a lot to you when—" she hesitated a heartbeat "—when we were seeing each other."

Seeing each other. Images of her flashed through his mind—Lilah lying on his bed, her hair spread against the sheets, the play of moonlight on her skin, the feel of her hand gliding down his abs and lower still… Best not to dwell on that. He cleared his throat.

"Can't help wondering if your dad might have changed his, er, business model. He wouldn't be the first to switch from moonshine to marijuana. That's where the real money is these days."

Gray eyes flashed. "You asking if Dad was a dope dealer? No way."

There was no kind way to have her face the possibility. Might as well be honest. "There's been rumors. We know for a fact that there's a huge drug-running operation that passes through our mountains. We just haven't been able to make a major bust yet."

"Rumors?" She stood and paced, temper sparking in

her clipped movements. "Figures. Anything criminal happening in Elmore County and people are going to bring up Dad's name. It's so unfair. He never hurt anybody. And he never sold liquor to the teenagers that came around. Said moonshine was a grown man's drink."

Harlan bit the inside of his mouth to keep from blurting his thoughts. He'd liked Chauncey, but Lilah had either forgotten her dad's more violent tendencies or she'd shoved them to the back of her mind. She hadn't been especially close to her dad, but his death was so recent, so fresh in her heart, and Chauncey *was* her father, after all.

"I'm not judging him," Harlan said, treading lightly. "He had plenty of good qualities—a loyal friend, always minded his own business and generous to a fault. But he had a dark side, too. Chauncey spent many a night as a guest of the Elmore County jail for assault."

She shrugged. "Drunken bar fights."

Fierce fights that had resulted in serious injuries to the unlucky, foolhardy men who crossed him. But he let that pass without comment. "You've never seen anything else suspicious?"

"I know what pot plants look like. If I'd seen any on our property, I'd have reported it. Take a look around for yourself if you don't believe me."

"Your father didn't have to be growing it in his fields to participate. He could have managed an indoor operation."

"I don't know anything about that." Lilah crossed her arms.

If she had a fault, it was stubbornness. She'd come by it honestly as Chauncey Tedder's daughter. That man refused to live life on anyone else's terms and abided by his own creed of what constituted right and wrong—the law be damned. Truth be told, many mountain folk felt the same.

"If you find anything incriminating while you're staying here, I hope you'll tell me."

"Outlaws keeping a step ahead of the law up here?" she quipped. "Imagine that."

Were they ever. Every drug raid ended the same—a dead end with no evidence or suspects in sight. "This is serious, Lilah. Drug operations bring in a dangerous criminal element. They aren't like your dad."

She sobered. "Which is why Dad would never have been a part of that. *Never.*"

He raised his hands, palms out. "Okay, okay. I just can't help worrying about you staying out here alone."

"I won't be here long. There's no reason to stay now that…you know." She let her words trail off.

Now that their relationship was over.

Again, it hung heavy in the air between them, weighing on his shoulders like a thick blanket. "When?"

"Soon," she answered dismissively.

He'd lost the right to question her more closely about her comings and goings. None of his business.

"I'm sorry," he said. "Sorry for—"

"Forget it." She thrust out her chin. "I have."

Had she? Had Lilah really moved on? Because he sure as hell hadn't. "Why don't you stay with Darla while you're here? The next guy coming along to buy 'shine might not be as nice as the one that just skedaddled off your property."

He caught the slight tightness at the edge of her eyes.

"She's busy with Ed and her kids. We'd get on each other's nerves after a while, anyway."

"Too bad Jimmy couldn't have stayed longer."

"Yeah. He looked so sad when he had to fly back," she said wistfully.

His old friend, her brother, was no longer the free-spirited kid that he used to hang around with in high school—and occasionally get in trouble with. Jimmy's tour in Afghanistan had changed his carefree attitude. At the funeral, and even afterward, he'd been distant and grave. Shell-shocked, some might say.

The loud rumble of a diesel engine roared from the driveway, and Harlan stepped out onto the porch in time to see a large gruff man at the wheel. He sharply turned the truck, and it circled the yard before heading back down the road.

"Your cruiser is running off my dad's business," Lilah said drily.

He rubbed his chin. "Wish I could leave it here overnight."

"I'll be fine. Just go." With that, she turned away.

He'd been dismissed, and there wasn't a damn thing he could do about it. "At least for tonight, call your sister and see if she'll stay out here with you." At the cold snap of her gray eyes, he added, "Please."

"Maybe."

The old oak door shut firmly behind her. Stubborn woman.

A LEATHER CORDED bracelet with a crimson stone, a triple-stranded necklace of multicolored glass and a tarnished silver ring with a fake cameo carving. Lilah laid the jewelry on the kitchen table and examined the pieces. They obviously held little, if any, monetary value, but they'd been carefully wrapped in an embroidered linen handkerchief inside a red silk drawstring pouch. So they'd meant something to somebody at one time.

Curious, she'd called Mom, who'd snorted when asked if they'd once belonged to her. "Anything I wanted from that cabin, which wasn't much, I took with me when I left your dad." She also claimed never to have seen the jewelry. "Might have belonged to Chauncey's mama, but if it did, I never noticed he had them, and he never mentioned it to me. Your dad wasn't exactly the sentimental type, anyway."

Still, Lilah was reluctant to chuck the pieces in the charity box with everything else worth salvaging. If the jewelry had belonged to Granny Tedder, she wanted to keep it.

At the crunch of gravel outside, she peered out the front window. Good, just Darla and Uncle Thad come to call. She opened the screen door and waved them inside. Uncle Thad hefted Darla's overnight bag from the truck bed as her sister minced her way to the porch in high heels. Lilah suppressed a giggle. Even as a kid, Darla was into playing dress up and acting like a Hollywood ingenue instead of a hillbilly's daughter.

"Thanks for coming over, y'all. Harlan was over earlier and got me all paranoid about staying alone out here."

"Harlan, huh? He's sexy." Darla winked as she entered, leaving a trail of perfume in her wake.

Lilah ignored the comment.

"Got yer shotgun, don't ya?" Uncle Thad bellowed. "Yer safe enough." He huffed and puffed up the porch steps. He was a giant of a man, over six feet tall, and as strong and as broad-boned as an ox.

He always knew just what to say to make her feel better. She hugged him as he entered the cabin.

Darla walked to the kitchen table, hips swaying. When she pulled out a chair and sat, she crossed her legs, exposing a long stretch of thigh. "You've been working hard. I've never seen Dad's place look so tidy. At least not since Mama ran off." She tossed her hair and sighed. "Be a love and make me a cup of coffee. Those kids 'bout ran me ragged today."

Lilah exchanged a quick knowing glance with Uncle Thad, who was dragging the suitcase to the back bedroom. Somehow, everything always centered on Darla and her needs. Feeling guilty, Lilah set about fixing the coffee. After all, her sister was busy with her own home life and didn't have to come babysit a grown fraidy-cat woman.

"What do we have here?" Darla cooed, picking up the multicolored necklace and holding it to the light.

"Found them under Dad's mattress. Any idea who they belong to?"

"No, but it's mine now." Darla clasped the necklace around her neck and preened. "How does it look?"

Gaudy, actually. Lilah measured the coffee and started the machine. "Mmm," she said noncommittally.

Uncle Thad waved from the den. "Gotta hit the road. Momma's waiting dinner on me."

"Tell Aunt Vi I said hey," Lilah called from the kitchen.

Darla put on the bracelet and ring. "Not too shabby, I guess. Whatcha think, Uncle?"

He stopped and stared. "Where'd ya get those baubles?"

"Lilah found them. Do they look pretty on me?"

"Sure, sure. Not that you need adornment." He winked at Lilah. Uncle Thad knew how to flatter his niece.

"You want to keep one, Lilah?" Darla asked.

"Nah, that's okay. They should go to someone who appreciates them."

Uncle Thad left, and Lilah warmed up a large pot of chicken and dumplings and another pot of butter beans. She was suddenly ravenous and exhausted as the aroma kicked in, and she absently stirred the dumplings, thinking of all the things she'd have loved to discuss with Darla. Hidden matters of the heart. But there was a layer of reserve between them. It seemed sometimes as if Darla resented her. Lilah had left Lavender Mountain years ago, finished her high school degree, and would soon graduate college with her teacher's certificate, whereas Darla had never left, never finished her schooling and had pretty much been forced into marriage when she'd gotten pregnant at sixteen.

Lilah set their plates on the table and sat across from her. "I know the kids keep you busy, but aren't they fun, too? I mean, you like being a mother, don't you?"

Darla shrugged. "It has its moments, I suppose. But it's lots of work. More than I realized it would be."

"But satisfying, right?"

"Sure," she said carelessly, lifting her little finger as she sipped her coffee.

Well, that hadn't been particularly enlightening or encouraging. What had she expected? Lilah ate, savoring the homemade food. As soon as her stomach was sated, lethargy crept in like a drug. She blinked, surveying the dirty dishes with dread. All she wanted was to crawl into bed and snuggle under the covers.

"Hey, kid." Darla's hand closed over hers. "You look beat. I'll wash the dishes."

"You will?" She couldn't keep the surprise out of her voice.

"Of course. You go on to bed."

Beat didn't even begin to cover how exhausted she felt. For the first time since she was a little kid, Lilah had begun taking afternoon naps. "I'll take you up on that offer," she said.

Darla slipped off the leather bracelet and clasped it around Lilah's wrist. "And you keep this. Stand up for yourself now and then, girl."

Unexpected tears gathered in her eyes, and she blinked them back. Every once in a blue moon, Darla surprised her. Nodding, she got up from the table and went to the bedroom. Without bothering to change into her nightgown, she slipped between the covers and fell into the black abyss of sleep.

COLD.

Lilah rubbed the goose bumps on her arm. Wind rustled through the pines and whooshed into the cabin.

Darla must have opened a window, she surmised, clambering out of bed.

The scrape of a heavy boot on the wooden floor brought her to an abrupt halt. The back of her neck prickled. Another step creaked in the hallway, and her mind raced. The shotgun was by the front door, so that was of no use. She hesitated, torn between locking her door or opening her bedroom window and hightailing it into the dark night.

But she couldn't leave Darla alone to face the menace.

Lilah unplugged the lamp on her nightstand and wrapped her hand around the base like a club. Not much of a weapon, but it was better than nothing. She stepped into the hallway and flattened herself against the wall, letting her eyes adjust to the dark.

Moonbeams cast a silvery glow in the den, and the shadows shifted, forming the silhouette of a man in black. He wasn't aware of her presence and crept from the rocking chair to the coffee table, picking up magazines and searching for…something. Did others know about the large amount of cash her father had stockpiled in the cabin? This could get ugly, deadly even. Maybe someone who'd been searching for the money had murdered her dad. Damn it, Harlan was right to warn her away from this place. Darla spending the night calmed her fears, but unless her sister was packing heat, she was of no help.

Lilah peeled herself away from the wall and stepped into the hallway to warn Darla of the danger. At the slight sound, the man straightened and spun around.

He had no face. Where eyes and nose and mouth should have been, there was nothing but inchoate blackness.

Lilah's pulse pounded furiously in her taut body. It was a nightmare come to life—paralysis rooted her feet to the floor and she could hardly breathe. The scream in her throat choked her lungs, refusing to unloose in the deathly quiet.

Suddenly, the intruder turned and ran for the open window.

A piercing cry vibrated her ears and brain. It took several seconds before she realized it was her own voice screaming. She stumbled to the front of the cabin on numb feet and dropped the lamp on the sofa, exchanging porcelain for the cold steel of the shotgun's barrel. A bolt of courage rippled down her spine, and she raced to the window and slammed it shut.

"What the hell is going on?" Darla rushed into the room and flipped on the light switch, revealing her baby doll nightie with its feathered neckline. Her mouth was devoid of the usual red lipstick, but pink sponge curlers dangled loosely in her brown hair. Oddly enough, the scanty attire only made her appear like an adolescent. A vulnerable, confused teenager.

"Somebody broke in. Did you open the window in here before you went to bed?"

"No. Is that how they got in? Did you get a good look at him?"

"He wore a mask."

"Oh, my God. I'm calling Ed to get out here."

"No sense rousing him and your kids out of bed. The man's gone."

"Are you crazy? I'm not staying here."

"We could drive into town and stay at a motel. But I don't relish the thought of going outside to get in the car."

"Call your Harlan. Tell him to get here ASAP."

Her Harlan. She wished he was. Not the mean, stupid Harlan who'd dumped her but the old Harlan who couldn't keep his hands off her and whose kisses had made her feel wild and cherished. She lifted her chin. "No. I won't bother him."

"Bother him? Isn't responding to break-ins, like, his *job*?"

She could call someone else in the sheriff's office, but Harlan would get word and come immediately. Lilah thought fast. "We could call Uncle Thad."

Darla grumbled. "Okay. But the only reason I'm not calling Ed is 'cause I don't wanna put my kids in danger."

"I'll make the call while you get dressed."

Darla sped to the bedroom, mumbling under her breath—something about the crazy gene in their family, Lilah thought.

Lilah grabbed the cell phone and punched in her uncle's number with her left hand, still clutching the gun in her right. She turned off the overhead light and stood by the window. Was he out there in the darkness, waiting for another night, another opportunity?

She would never feel safe here again. Maybe Harlan was right. Maybe Dad had gotten mixed up in some new dangerous scheme. A new gamble, a new adventure— one that had cost him his life. Who knew what desperate secrets lived in another's heart? She had to think about her own future, her own sad secret.

As soon as she'd settled her dad's affairs, she would leave Lavender Mountain.

Chapter Three

This was going to kill Darla.

She'd put off bringing up the matter of the missing money, imagining Darla's furious reaction at the news. For the past couple of days, she'd stayed tied up with all the paperwork concerning the robbery and fixing up Dad's old place. Darla was much too busy to be bothered. Okay, that wasn't entirely true or fair—she'd been avoiding this scene with her sister.

Tired as she was from the drama and all her duties, Lilah couldn't up and leave the mountain without letting her sister know the money was gone. She sped down Dark Corners Road to the homestead where Darla, Ed and their three children lived. Her sister would be devastated about the stolen money. If only she'd just let her have it that morning like Darla had begged. And she could kiss goodbye that sisterly chat she'd planned on. After the news, Darla would be in no mood to offer advice and comfort over the matter that had weighed on Lilah for weeks. It wasn't like there'd been much chance of Darla being supportive, anyway, if she was being honest with herself.

At the last sharp bend before hitting town, she pulled into Darla and Ed's gravel driveway. An unfamiliar red pickup truck was parked near the side porch. Maybe Ed had traded in his old clunker. She picked her way through a barrage of mangy dogs and mewling cats that barked or hissed their displeasure at the invasion of their territory.

Old toys and broken furniture almost barricaded the doorway, and she impatiently scooted a rusted table out of her path. Through the screen door she heard Darla talking on the phone.

"Yes, I'll hold. But only for a minute. Longer than that and I'll take my business elsewhere," Darla huffed.

Lilah pushed open the door and entered the kitchen where her sister held a tape measure stretched across the lower cabinets. "You back, sir? I want mahogany," Darla said. "Only the best. And I want it pronto."

Lilah blinked. Wow. This was a change. Ed must have been working overtime.

Darla retracted the tape and scribbled on a scrap sheet of paper, her face puckered in concentration.

"New cabinets, huh? Nice."

Her sister snapped her head up, pencil poised. "What are you doing here?"

Not the welcome she'd expected. But then, she and Darla had never been particularly close. The ten-year age difference was large enough so that shortly after their parents' divorce, a pregnant Darla had married Ed while Lilah had moved over a hundred miles away with their mother.

"Well, I'm leaving, and I thought I'd say goodbye first."

Darla colored slightly. "Right. Sorry I couldn't help out more with the estate stuff. Ed Junior's been down with a tummy ache."

"No problem." Lilah shrugged and waited awkwardly.

"I'll just, uh, get off the phone. Want something to drink?"

"Water, thanks." Lilah plopped down on a chair in the den.

The TV blared, although no one was watching it. Where were her nephews?

Darla returned from the kitchen and tossed her a water bottle. "Where are the kids?" Lilah asked.

"I started them in daycare yesterday. I needed more peace and quiet 'round here." She shuddered. "I'm still recovering from that intruder scare."

"Me, too," Lilah admitted. "I meant it when I said I'm not staying. I'll come back when there's papers that need to be signed when the cabin sells, and for the meeting next week in the probate office."

Darla tossed back her hair. "Both stupid formalities. That cabin's not worth much, and I doubt Dad had more than a few hundred dollars in the bank. A complete waste of time."

"But he had thirty thousand dollars lying around the house," she pointed out.

"Dad didn't trust banks. Besides, I bet he was just holding that money for someone."

Lilah suppressed a shudder. If that was true, was that why the intruder had been in the cabin? Would he return?

"Anyway, do you think you could take care of all the

paperwork for me?" Lilah asked hesitantly. "I only got involved with everything because Jimmy was overseas and you said you were too busy with the kids to fool with it. Now that they're in daycare…maybe you could take over?"

"You handle it. You always were good with all that complicated kind of stuff."

Irritation flared between her temples. "But I live over a hundred miles from here, and I'm busy, too."

"You?" Darla scoffed. "You don't have other people depending on you to feed them and watch over them. Or a demanding husband. What else do you have to do?"

That about hit her last reserve of patience. "I have a j-o-b. Remember? I also take college classes in whatever spare time I have."

"Pfft." Darla waved a hand dismissively. "Why you wasting time getting a fancy degree…"

But Lilah tuned out her words. Instead, she was mesmerized by the huge diamond flashing on Darla's left hand. "Ed upgraded your wedding ring? It used to be on the small side." Rinky-dink was more like it.

Darla abruptly lowered her hand and crossed her arms, hiding the ring from view.

The new pickup, ordering new cabinets, fancy jewelry. Well, that little mystery was solved.

"It was you!" Lilah stood and pointed her finger. "You're the one who stole the money."

"It wasn't *stealing*. That was Dad's money, and I'm sure he meant for me to have it."

Of all the selfishness Lilah had witnessed over the

years with her sister, this was the most outrageous. "All for you, huh? What about me and Jimmy?"

"Jimmy's making plenty of money in the army."

"And me?"

"You're about to become a teacher. You'll be rolling in dough. I need it more than you. I have a family. You don't."

Lilah closed her eyes, thinking of how much thirty thousand dollars would have helped in paying off her college tuition and upgrading from her clinker of a car to something more reliable. Rolling in dough on a teacher's salary? Not hardly.

She drew a long steadying breath. "We'll see what Jimmy thinks about all this when I call him tonight."

"Do you have to tell him?" Darla flushed and bit her lip. "We ain't spent it all yet. I could give you each a few thousand."

She'd never been so angry. Lilah trembled from the injustice. *Careful, careful. Don't say something you'll regret.* "I'll see you later, after I've spoken with Jimmy," she said past numb lips.

"Ah, come on, LayLay," Darla cajoled, using her old childhood nickname. "Don't get all mad on me."

Lilah strode past her, eager to avoid more confrontation. "We'll settle up after I talk to Jimmy. I'll be speaking with Harlan, too. He knows that money was stolen from the cabin. I'm sure he'll want to question you about the theft."

Darla paled. "Now, look here…"

"Save it for the cops," Lilah said, marching out of the house and back to her car. Of all the nerve. Of course, she wasn't going to press charges, but let Darla sweat it a little.

Inside her car, she backed out of the driveway and then paused. Go left or right? Left meant leaving the mountain, right meant having "The Talk" with Harlan. She dreaded it, but her conscience demanded she tell him. Besides, he'd already called, wanting her to sign the missing money report.

Digging deep into her reserves of courage, Lilah turned right.

THE MOMENTARY LULL in the crowded, noisy sheriff's office alerted Harlan that something was off. He glanced up from his paperwork and followed the gaze of his co-workers to the front door.

Ah, yes. Lilah Tedder had that effect on the opposite sex. She turned her head, scanning the room until she zeroed in on where he sat. Her blond hair glowed like a halo under the harsh fluorescent lighting, but her eyes burned like two flames, hot and flickering.

She was no angel.

Lilah beelined to his desk in determined steps. He hoped J.D. wouldn't come out of his office anytime soon this morning and witness them together. She stepped up to his chair.

"So you've already drawn up the report on the money?" she asked, cutting to the chase.

"Yep." Harlan picked up the printed document. "Just need you to sign it."

She sat down next to him and primly placed her purse in her lap. He slid the paper toward her, and she glanced down. "I'm not signing it. There's no longer any need for a report."

"Why? You found it?"

"In a manner of speaking, yes."

He was missing something. People didn't "misplace" thousands of dollars of cash. "That's good. Where was it?"

"I forgot I'd moved it from under the mattress to the bottom dresser drawer."

She was lying, but why? Truth was, he'd been reluctant to write up the report, not wanting to draw unnecessary attention to her newfound wealth. At least not until the money was accounted for and safely deposited in the bank. Besides, her family's name was mud as it was. This report would drag more fodder and speculation about Chauncey's questionable activities.

"Are you sure about this? What's really going on?"

"I'm more worried about intruders than…"

She stopped, obviously flustered about blurting out that tidbit.

"Intruders?" he honed in quickly. "You have any more men showing up to buy moonshine?"

"No. Never mind about that. I'm leaving today, anyway."

"Sure you won't change your mind?" He'd secretly hoped she would hang around long enough for him to try to win her back.

"It's for the best."

"You're scared. Tell me what's going on. Has someone hurt you or threatened you in any way?" If they had, he'd hunt them down like a dog and make them pay. He lowered his voice and took her hand. "Tell me."

She jerked her hand away. "There's nothing to tell. Forget the report."

"Sure, never mind that I wasted an hour writing this up," he shot back, hurt and annoyed.

Lilah shrugged. "Sorry."

Her tone implied she was anything but sorry.

"For God's sake, Lilah, what the hell is going on here?" He was conscious of his fellow officers glancing their way. He lowered his voice. "First, the missing money, then you hint at an intruder and now you deny anything's wrong?"

"Don't badger me, Harlan Sampson," she said, glaring. "I didn't come here today to talk about the report, anyway. That's not important."

"Not important?" he asked, incredulous. "Are you for real? I demand to know what's going on."

She jumped to her feet, her face flushed and her voice raised. "You have no right to demand anything from me. Never did. I just dropped by to tell you that I'm—I'm... oh, never mind. I won't bother you with the news."

The room was the quietest Harlan had ever witnessed. From deep in the recesses behind their administrative offices, an inmate could be heard cursing in a holding cell.

This wasn't happening. His mind spun in circles. Surely Lilah wasn't about to say she was pregnant, was she? They'd been careful. Except, well, there were a couple of times they'd been too impatient. He felt like he'd fallen down into a deep well and couldn't catch his breath.

Lilah raised her chin and strolled away, her back ramrod stiff. From the corner of his eyes, he caught Sheriff Bentley shaking his head in an I-told-you-so way.

Instead of heading to the front door, she made an abrupt turn to the right and entered the women's restroom. Jolene Smithers, a fellow officer, rose from behind her desk. "I'll check on her," she said, eyes wide with equal measures of pity and curiosity.

To hell with J.D.

He found his feet and followed Jolene, aware that every eye in the room was upon them. Someone snickered, and the back of his neck flushed with heat.

LILAH PULLED BACK her hair and leaned over the toilet, gagging. A few deep, shuddering breaths later, she straightened, bracing her hands against the stall's cool metal siding.

That'd been close. For a moment back there, she'd been ready to upchuck all over Harlan's carefully prepared report. One that was no longer needed.

"Get yourself together and get the hell out of Dodge," she muttered.

"You all right in there?" a female voice drawled.

Lilah stiffened. "I'm fine," she said in a mind-your-own-business tone.

"Don't sound fine to me."

Lilah waited. Whoever was on the other side of the door wasn't leaving and wasn't entering the neighboring stall. Just what she needed. Why couldn't a girl get a clean break when she needed to beat a hasty exit? Sighing, she pushed open the door and strode to the washbasin, determined to ignore the nosy stranger. From the corner of her eye, she took her in—a tall rangy woman, wearing a brown uniform and a badge.

"Quite a scene out there," the woman commented drily.

Lilah splashed her face and rinsed her mouth out.

"I think Harlan's worried about you."

"Told ya I was fine." She jerked a paper towel from the dispenser and dried her face and hands before throwing it in the bin.

"You with child?" the woman asked.

Lilah snatched the keys from her pocketbook and marched to the door. Another minute and she would be out of this stifling place.

"Is it Harlan's?"

The nerve. Lilah's eyes snapped to meet the intruder's. She wore no makeup and her auburn hair was pulled back in a careless ponytail. Still, it was easy to see she was a beauty in a tomboyish, no-frills kind of way with a peaches-and-cream complexion and large hazel eyes.

"None of your business…" Lilah glanced at the nameplate pinned below her badge. "Officer Smithers."

"We're all good buddies working here. Family, even. So is it his?"

Lilah pushed past the woman but Jolene Smithers stepped in front of her.

"Following in your sister's footsteps? Guess I should give you some credit, though. At least you managed to finish high school before populating our county with more Tedders."

The *hell*? It may have been years since she'd lived in

Lavender Mountain, but Smithers's lip curl of disgust when she said *Tedders* slashed through time. Once again, Lilah was young and facing the taunts of schoolchildren or braving the slights of classmates who never came to her birthday parties. No parent wanted their child hanging out with the likes of Lilah and her family.

"Get out of my way," she said coldly.

"I'm betting it isn't. Good thing we have paternity tests these days. Keeps riffraff like you from tying down a decent man who—no doubt—will insist on doing the right thing. Either marriage or child support for the next eighteen years."

Jolene's words splattered like acid on Lilah's heart. That much was true. Harlan would insist on doing right by her. But what kind of life would that be—knowing she'd unwittingly trapped him into marriage? He couldn't know the truth.

"And what about his career?" Jolene continued. "He'd be the laughing stock of this county, running for sheriff after a shotgun wedding to a Tedder."

She'd had enough. Lilah went around Jolene and flung open the restroom's door before delivering her parting shot as she stepped into the lobby. "It's not his baby. Okay? You happy now?"

Whipping her head back around, she faced a tall uniformed column of stubborn human male.

Harlan.

His feet were planted less than six feet from the doorway and his face was set like carved granite.

How much had he heard? He couldn't have missed her saying the baby wasn't his. Lilah lowered her head and walked quickly to the door. She'd come by to tell him she was pregnant with his child, but maybe it was best this way.

So why was she near tears? If he had ever loved her, that love hadn't been enough to erase the stigma of her name. Believing she was pregnant by another man, so quickly after their own affair had ended, would be proof to him that she was fickle and unworthy.

OUTSIDE, THE GEORGIA sun beat down like a whip on his face. "Lilah. Stop." He placed a hand on her shoulder, and she froze. He stepped in front of her and gazed at her pale face. Now that he had her attention, he hadn't a clue what to say.

"Sorry you heard the news that way," she said flatly. "Didn't want you to wonder if it was yours, though— just in case we ran into each other in the future or you heard something."

"Are you sure?" he asked. This didn't feel right.

"Positive."

Anger churned his gut. There hadn't been anyone else for him since he'd cut off ties with Lilah. How had she moved on so quickly? "Who?" he ground out past numb lips.

Her brows raised and she regarded him blankly.

"Who's the father?"

"Oh. You don't know him. He's not from around here."

She was lying. He was—almost—sure of it.

"Is the baby mine or not? I deserve the truth."

She hesitated. "You deserve a life with a woman you love. You deserve to be sheriff."

"Is that what this is about? Let me decide what I want."

"Do you love me?" she asked abruptly.

His mind drew a blank. Love? He cared for her... *mightily* cared. But love? "I... I'm..."

Her lips trembled, and she pinched them together. "Whatever happened between us is long over. I have to figure things out on my own."

"You shouldn't have to face this alone. What about this...this other man?" His mind whirled at the possibility she was telling the truth. "Will he marry you? Or at least support you?"

She gave a harsh laugh. "The days of shotgun weddings 'round these parts are long over. Plenty of women have been single moms. I can do the same."

A memory pierced him—her dad at the Foxy Lady bar/motel, hunting down Ed after getting word that Darla was with child. By all witness accounts, Chauncey had stormed into the dive, red-faced and waving a shotgun, searching for the hapless culprit who'd deflowered his eldest daughter. Seeing Ed shirk into the corner, Chauncey had approached and grabbed a fistful of Ed's camouflage jacket. "Congratulations, you're getting married," he'd announced.

Harlan ran a finger over the collar rim of his stiff uniform shirt. Those days of forced marriages weren't entirely over. Chauncey Tedder would be mighty displeased about this situation if he were still alive. He cleared his throat. "But you don't have to raise a child alone if he—"

"Just go back to work, Harlan. This is my problem, not yours." She darted around him, but not quickly enough for him to miss the tears brimming in her eyes.

"Are you going to be okay driving home?" he asked. Damn it, he still cared about her even though he shouldn't.

She didn't bother responding. Instead, she climbed in her car and backed out of the parking space a tad too carelessly. She whipped out of the lot and accelerated onto the highway. Within a minute, the car disappeared in the distance.

It was as if Lilah couldn't wait to be rid of him.

"She gone?" Jolene was suddenly beside him.

"Looks that way."

"It's for the best, Harlan." She ran a hand along his arm. "Time you moved on. If you ever want to talk, I'm here."

He frowned and moved out of her reach. This wasn't Jolene's first hint she wanted something more than friendship.

"Plenty of other fish in the sea." She smiled and practically batted her eyes.

But he had zero interest in his comely coworker. Instead of a tall redhead, his interest was decidedly marked in favor of a certain petite blonde. One who clearly was over him and might even be pregnant with another man's baby.

So why was he so upset? Hadn't that been what he wanted all along—a clean break with Lilah? But he walked away from Jolene and headed back to work weighted with a heaviness that made him feel suddenly ten years older.

Chapter Four

Harlan considered himself lucky. Today would be so busy that thoughts of Lilah would be temporarily relegated to the back burner. Last night had been a tough and fitful sleep—was the baby his or not and why should he care?—but after numerous cups of coffee, he now had enough stamina to get through the day's scheduled raid.

He and five other officers surrounded the abandoned older home. Kudzu crept over the windows like a living, breathing veil. So convenient for anyone hiding illegal drugs. One would expect to see broken windows and doors in a vacated building, but for all its age and the superficial facade of neglect, the front door was bolted shut with a steel chain and padlock and it lacked signs of forced entry anywhere.

Not only that but also dozens of large footsteps had tamped down the overgrown grass and weeds surrounding the house. They'd been there when he and the team had arrived.

He had a good feeling about this one.

Remote homes sprinkled Appalachia, but this place on top of Booze Mountain took the cake. It had taken them a good half an hour of driving up increasingly narrow and bumpy dirt roads to get here.

Sammy Armstrong sidled over and gave him a broad wink. "How's your girlfriend doing?"

Harlan gritted his teeth. If it had been someone other than his old childhood friend teasing him, he would have busted his chops. "Fine," he spat, not inviting further conversation.

Sammy nudged him. "Lilah's more than fine. A real looker. A man could do worse."

J.D. pulled into the lot and exited the cruiser, patting his uniform shirt pocket. "I got the subpoena. Let's do this."

Alvin Lee, a fellow officer, marched up the sagging porch steps with a pair of giant bolt cutters.

Harlan idly swatted at a skeeter that buzzed near his ear and swiped his arm across his sweaty forehead. The heat was brutal, even up here in the mountains.

The chain crashed onto the wooden porch with a clatter nearly as loud as a shotgun blast. Alvin kicked in the door, and Harlan followed him inside the abandoned home.

The stench of stale food pervaded—a toxic mixture of fried bologna and venison. In the center of the main room, the scratched surface of a long table was littered with boxes, string and packing tape. It looked like an assembly line set up. Easy to guess the sort of merchandise packaged here.

He glanced around the mostly ruined interior, and his spirits sank. It looked deserted. Not even a single marijuana plant in sight. So much for his intuition.

Three other officers entered via the back door, and J.D. strolled into the room, thumbs tucked into his belt. "Find any drugs?" he asked hopefully.

Harlan swiped a finger on the fine layer of white powder on the table. Much too white for mere dust. "Probably cocaine residue," he answered, brushing off the powder on his pant legs. "Afraid that's going to be the extent of our find."

"Damn it. Not again." J.D. stalked off to the adjacent kitchen. "Comb the area for leftover receipts, matches— anything left behind that might give us some clue who's been here."

Sammy slammed his fist into his open palm. "What is this? Almost a half dozen raids now in the last year? They're always a step ahead of us." He huffed in frustration. "It's like they know we're coming."

Dread settled in Harlan's gut as he assimilated the words. He didn't want to believe it. They were a small team, and he'd grown up with most of them on the mountain. They were his friends, his colleagues, the people he trusted in dangerous situations.

But the lure of easy money could mess with a person's mind. He'd seen it before. A younger officer, Caleb, had fallen into that trap last year. First, it was turning a blind eye on minor offenses like illegal poker games. Then it progressed to fixing tickets for family and friends. Word spread until it reached a point where everyone believed they could offer a little money in return for a favor, muddying boundaries. Even if he'd wanted to stop taking bribes, Caleb had confessed that if he *hadn't* taken them, someone would have squealed.

Someone always squealed. You could count on that. It held true for inmates as well as the officers who were supposed to enforce the law.

In the end, Caleb had been fired.

Harlan tapped a finger against his lips. Caleb still dated Marla, one of the two dispatchers on the day shift. Did Marla pump him with information on their scheduled raids? Mentally, he made a note to check on that.

J.D.'s cell phone rang, and he tossed it on the kitchen counter. "Answer that while I help Alvin search the back bedroom."

Harlan picked it up. "Sampson here," he said, opening a drawer and searching its sparse contents as Marla breathlessly reported the latest news.

Another shooting. Another victim dead.

An icy finger of fear shimmied down his spine. Lilah— and their baby—might be in danger.

LILAH RUBBED HER swollen eyes, then riffled through the stack of bills that had collected in her mailbox during her absence. Absentmindedly going up the stairs, she almost ran smack into Luke McCoy at the bottom of the apartment stairwell.

"Whoa there, missy," he said with a laugh. "We missed you while you were gone." She glanced up, and his easy grin melted away. "You all right?"

Lilah gave him a watery smile. "I'm fine."

"You don't look fine. Need a friend? We could talk over breakfast and coffee."

Sure, but she hated to encourage the guy. He'd been

asking her out for weeks now, and if she went out with him, he'd make a big deal of it.

"No, really. It was a rough night, but I'm okay."

"Missing your family, I bet," he said knowingly. "Ms. Cranston told me you went home for your father's funeral and stayed awhile to take care of the estate and stuff."

She made a mental note to be more circumspect with her elderly neighbor. "Right," she agreed, clutching at the excuse.

A brown-and-white cop cruiser whipped into a nearby parking spot, and she idly watched as a man got out. He locked the door and turned, rapidly making his way toward them. It couldn't be. A familiar shock of brown hair, a strong jaw and piercing blue eyes… Yes, it was Harlan. What was he doing here? And dressed in his uniform, too?

"I think breakfast is just what you need," Luke continued, unaware of Harlan approaching from behind. "Let me take you out."

Her stomach revolted at the thought of food. "No, thank you."

"Ah, come on—"

"The lady said no," Harlan snapped.

"What are you doing here?" she asked.

His jaw tightened. "We have business to discuss."

Luke held up a hand and shuffled backward. "I'll leave you two alone then."

Well, at least he might not pester her for dates anymore. So at least something good would come of this unexpected meeting with Harlan.

"Is that him?" Harlan asked stiffly.

"What? Oh, you mean… Never mind, it's still none of your business."

"Seemed pretty spineless to me," Harlan observed. "He cut out pretty quick when I came."

"You practically ordered him to leave," she argued. "Besides—"

"Yoo-hoo, officer!" They looked up the stairs, where Ms. Cranston stood in her housecoat. "That was quick. I just called five minutes ago."

"Ma'am, I'm not—"

"I got to puzzling on that stranger hanging around here last night, and the more I thought on it, the more scared I got on account of—"

"Stranger?" Harlan took the stairs two at a time and withdrew a small notebook from his shirt pocket. "When? What did he look like?"

Lilah followed him, trying to quell the butterflies of alarm in her stomach.

"He was medium height, a little on the thin side and dressed all in black. Kept walking back and forth in that hallway there." She pointed to the hall where Lilah's apartment was.

"Did he wear a black ski mask?" Lilah asked, holding her breath.

"No. If he had, I'd a called the police right away."

"Could you describe his face or hair?" Harlan asked.

Ms. Cranston shook her head. "He stayed in the shadows."

Harlan sighed and returned the notepad to his shirt pocket.

"Thing is," Ms. Cranston continued, "another feller

came 'round this morning dressed all in black. I leaned out my window and yelled, 'Hey, whatcha doin'?' He took off running to the parking lot without even turning around to see who was talking."

"Did you get a look at the car make and model, or a tag?"

"It was a big dark blue car," she said. "Sorry, I don't know models and such as that."

Harlan nodded. "Thank you, ma'am." He took Lilah's arm and motioned for the stairs.

"Hope you catch him," Ms. Cranston called to their backs. "I don't cotton to strangers roaming around here. Up to no good, I bet."

"We're going to your apartment, and you're going to pack your things," Harlan said in his no-nonsense voice. "We'll talk on the way to Lavender Mountain."

"WON'T BE ANY safer there," she muttered. Inside her apartment, she whirled to face him. "You can't just show up and start ordering me around."

His face was as set as she'd ever seen it. "Have a seat."

Something was wrong. *Bad* wrong. Her jellied legs no longer felt strong enough to support her weight, and she sank into the nearest chair, clasping her hands in her lap. "What's happened?"

Harlan ran a hand through his hair and sank to his knees beside her, so close she could feel the heat of his skin and inhale the scent of his woodsy aftershave. "There's no easy way to break this, darlin'."

Who was in trouble or hurt this time? Jimmy? He'd returned to his tour in Afghanistan last week, and Lord knew that he'd been placed in dangerous missions time and again—

"It's Darla," he said gently, placing a large rough hand over hers and squeezing. "She's been murdered."

No. *No, not her sister.* "I just saw her yesterday," she mumbled. How stupid. As if that meant Darla couldn't possibly be dead. Lilah shook off the useless denial. "How…"

"Shot in the back."

Murder again. The air pressed in and her lungs seized. She squeezed in a painful breath and exhaled. "Same as Dad?"

"Yes."

Without thinking, she collapsed onto his broad shoulders, her body shaking uncontrollably. *Not again. Not again.* Harlan shifted into the chair beside her and guided her onto his lap where she felt cradled by his strength. His hands rubbed up and down her back. She focused on his touch—it was all she could grasp to stop the maelstrom of mourning, which threatened to overwhelm her.

First Dad, and now Darla. All in the space of a week.

Lilah snapped her head up, remembering she wasn't alone in her grief. "Those poor kids! And Ed, too."

Harlan brushed away the tears on her cheek. "We've called Ed's parents, and they're on the way. If need be, they can keep the children at their place while we get to the bottom of this."

"Surely Ed wants them there with him. And I can go over and stay a bit until things settle down. Help him out. He must be devastated."

"You think so?"

"Of course." She cocked her head to the side, digesting the impact of his words. "You don't... I mean... You aren't saying *Ed* killed Darla, are you?"

"We're not ruling anything out. Usually, a killer is someone known intimately by the victim."

She tensed, fighting the sudden shudder that crawled up her spine. "Not in this case. It's the same way my dad was killed, so it must be the same person. And Ed had no beef with Dad."

"That you know of," Harlan corrected.

"Only when he got Darla pregnant in high school. Once they got married, Dad and Ed got along just fine."

"Did your brother-in-law ever work for your dad on the side?"

"Not that I'm aware of. Are you arresting Ed?"

"J.D.'s questioning him now."

She jumped off his lap. "And the kids? I have to get down there. They might need me." Guilt snaked its way through her gut, insidious and slimy. Who was she kidding? Nobody needed her. She and Darla had had a major argument over the stolen money. The last time she'd seen her sister, she'd stormed out of the house, threatening to put the cops on her tail.

Frantically, she grabbed her purse off the table, eager to leave and keep her mind and hands busy instead of dwelling on the news. "I've got to pack a few clothes, and...and..." She blindly stumbled into the coffee table and rubbed her shins.

"I'll drive you." Harlan took her purse and set it on

the sofa. "Go ahead and pack. Take your time. There's no rush."

She shook her head. "No. I'll need my own vehicle. I don't want to be dependent on you to drive me everywhere while I'm back."

"Yeah, about that. The easiest thing all around is for you to stay with me. Ed and the kids have his parents to help out, and there's no sense in you wasting money on a motel."

No. He didn't love her, and she wouldn't be a burden to him or anyone else. Lilah thought fast. There was always Uncle Thad and Aunt Vi, but with their eight children, it tended to be a bit noisy and cramped.

"I can stay with my Aunt Ruth who lives about forty miles from here. She has health problems so she'll appreciate my help around the house and my company." She stifled the impulse to cross her fingers behind her back. Ruth was nearly seventy years old and had never married or had children—a quiet woman like her preferred the solitary life. Yes, she'd recently had minor surgery but, truth be told, Ruth was just fine on her own.

His brow furrowed. "She doesn't have anyone else to take care of her? I don't like you working so hard."

"No. Besides, what's it to you?"

His eyes trailed down to her belly. "Somebody needs to look out for you."

Lilah couldn't help it. She blushed.

Harlan quirked a brow. "Since when have you ever been shy with me?"

Yeah, he was right about that. No point in modesty after he knew every inch of her body. Lilah shook off the sudden images of Harlan's intimate kisses. Now wasn't the time for remembering such things.

"I'll need to call the Red Cross again and get word to Jimmy."

"I can do it for you," Harlan volunteered.

"No. I'm family. I should." Lord, she didn't want to, though. Her brother had enough stress without hearing that yet another family member had been murdered.

"We'll do it together. Tonight."

Lilah wavered. It *would* be nice to stay with Harlan. There was nowhere she'd feel more protected. On the other hand, going to his place would stir up the old memories of the time they'd spent together. A happier time when she'd thought they'd be together forever.

Harlan obviously sensed her hesitation and moved in for the kill. "Come on," he said in his husky, sexy voice. "It'll give us an opportunity to talk. I'm still not convinced the baby isn't mine."

The baby. Lilah's hand went to her stomach. She had to consider more than just her own feelings. Harlan could protect her...protect *them*. It didn't mean they were a couple again. And there was no denying that she and all her family were in danger. This was far from over— something deep and rotten and evil lay at the bottom of these two deaths.

It was only a matter of time before the killer struck again.

Who would be next?

Chapter Five

"It's a formality."

Harlan placed his broad hand on the small of her back and guided her into the antiseptic, frigid forensics room located in the bowels of the county hospital.

Lilah's breath came in rapid, shallow bursts. *I can't do this.* She thought of Ed. He was always in the background at family gatherings, a quiet presence and foil to Darla's chatter and dramatics. A seemingly decent guy.

But now, the normally stoic Ed was barely holding himself together. His large hands were trembling by his sides.

I have to be here. It's the last kindness I can do for my sister. Help her family in their time of need.

"It will all be over in a minute," Harlan whispered reassuringly in her ear.

"Right." One quick glance, a thumbs-up to the coroner from Ed and she was out of there.

An older woman in pastel blue scrubs and a white coat nodded at her briskly, but not unkindly. Lilah's gaze dropped to the gurney where a body was draped over with a white sheet. Darla's body. She forced her leaden feet forward and nodded, glad Harlan's hand remained at the base of her spine. Ed groaned and then pinched his lips together in determination. Lilah patted his arm.

At his nod, the woman turned down the sheet with a practiced flick of her wrist.

Red lipstick blazed against pale alabaster skin tinged with a morgue-blue undertone. Dishwater-blond hair fell carelessly over stiff shoulders. The curve of her jaw and cheekbones, the delicate arch of her brows, a certain sculpting of the nose and lips—Lilah could see herself in the family genetics. Thank heavens they had only revealed her face. There was no hint of the violence she'd endured. But if rolled over, Darla's body would have been visibly marred by shotgun pellets.

The sheet was short on the left side and Lilah observed Darla's lifeless hand that peeked out from under the edge of the cover.

"It's her," Ed croaked. "Darla Marie Tedder Stovall."

The woman immediately pulled the sheet back over Darla, covering her face.

Harlan nodded to the technician. "Thank you, ma'am."

"The secretary out front will have you sign a paper confirming the identification. Sorry for your loss."

They were officially dismissed.

Lilah wanted to say goodbye to Darla, say she was sorry that sharp words were the last ones spoken between them. But it was too late. She swallowed the regret and walked out of the cold room, breathing deeply as they headed toward the desk. A young man handed them a clipboard and pen. "Sign here," he said, motioning to the signature line at the bottom of the sheet.

Ed scribbled his name with shaking hands.

"There's freshly brewed coffee," he offered them. "Can I get y'all a cup?"

Ed shook his head and looked up at the ceiling.

"Yes—I mean, no." She sure could use the comfort of warm caffeinated liquid, but her own needs were secondary for the next few months.

"How about some water?" Harlan asked her, his deep voice rumbling behind her.

"What I really want is to get out of here first."

Harlan nodded. "Thanks, but we're fine," he told the tech, ushering them to the elevator.

Once inside, Harlan pressed the button and they rumbled up to the main floor. Ed exhaled and scrubbed at his face.

She couldn't imagine the pain he must be in. "How are the kids doing this morning?" she said around the burn in her throat.

"Mom's watching them."

The elevator door opened and they emerged into the main lobby. The hustle and bustle seemed miles away from the stillness of the basement morgue. Ed walked out first, eyes blinking. He held out a hand to Lilah. "Thanks for coming in with me. It helped. I could tell Dad didn't want to do it."

She glanced over toward the patient waiting area where Ed's father slowly rose from a vinyl sofa and shuffled their way. "Understandable. Call me if there's anything I can do. Anything."

He nodded and she watched as he and his father exited the building into the beautiful, sun-shining day.

"It should be dark and stormy," she said, lips trembling. "And pouring down rain."

A nagging sense of unease quivered in the dark recesses of her brain, and she rubbed her temples. Something wasn't quite right about the viewing of Darla, other than the obvious.

"Headache?" Harlan asked.

"No. I can't explain it. But I feel like I'm missing some important detail. I looked at Darla and…" Her voice drifted off.

"It's been a shock. I should have insisted Ed do this himself."

"It would have only made things harder for him, and he needs to be strong for his kids. And it wasn't just seeing her dead. It's something else."

"I'll get you that water and we'll be on our way."

Alone, she regarded the preoccupied staff and visitors go about the business of living.

Harlan returned and pressed a bottle of water into her hands. Lilah sipped it tentatively. Not too bad, actually. It erased the lingering chill in her belly. "Maybe this will help me think better."

"Do you need to go back into the examining room?"

"Hope not. Let me sit here a spell and concentrate."

His hand was powerful and comforting as he guided her to an unused waiting room and onto a sofa. "Take your time. If you want, we can come back tomorrow and talk to the forensics doctor if you need to. No rush."

She didn't want to return and she didn't want to see

her sister's body again. *Think*. Lilah placed her head in her hands and reviewed the last few minutes as if she were a camera, detached and methodical, scanning the scene to replay it for details. She'd entered the morgue, blinking from the glaring whiteness of the fluorescent lights and the white walls. The technician had unrolled the white sheet, exposing Darla's face, and then she'd glimpsed Darla's left hand where the sheet had exposed her bare fingers curled at the edge of the metal gurney.

"That's it!" Lilah jerked her head up and snapped her fingers. "Darla wasn't wearing any jewelry. Not even her wedding ring."

"She always wore it?"

"Always."

Harlan didn't appear too impressed with her realization. "They might have removed all the jewelry before you saw her."

She hadn't considered that. They'd probably given Ed the wedding ring and the costume jewelry Darla had been wearing from the cabin.

"Why Darla?" she whispered, leaning her head against the cold hard wall. "Maybe Dad was involved in shady business. Even bigger than moonshine. Maybe even Ed and Uncle Thad and my boatload of cousins are as well. But Darla?"

"Women commit crimes, too—not that I'm saying your sister did."

She shook her head adamantly. Darla hadn't been concerned about anything past her own little world of her kids and her home. And she was much too lazy to get involved with work in any shape, form or fashion.

Lilah wanted to bite her tongue at the traitorous thought. Darla had plenty of good qualities like… Well, no need to make an inventory.

What kind of mess had her father dragged them all into? She would never feel safe again until the killer was captured. And now, she had a baby to protect as well.

HARLAN SHIFTED THE suitcases in his hands and glanced longingly at the master bedroom.

"Don't even think about it," Lilah said flatly. "I'll take the spare."

With a sigh, he walked across to the guest bedroom and set the suitcases at the foot of the bed. Things would certainly be less complicated without sex. "You know where the bathroom is. Anything else you need?"

"I'm good."

Her tone was rigid. So much for their brief moments of closeness during the day's crisis. He'd only been someone to lean on temporarily. Not that he blamed Lilah a bit. He deserved nothing but her mistrust after the way he'd disappeared from her life. And, apparently, she'd found another man soon afterward to take his place. Or so she claimed.

Awkwardly, he placed a hand on her tensed shoulder. "Sorry about Darla."

She nodded and averted her face, but not before he saw a well of tears threatening to spill over. "I'll just head to the shower now."

Lilah opened one of the suitcases and haphazardly rummaged, finally pulling out a pair of flowered cotton pajama shorts and a matching pink tank top. "Excuse me."

She brushed against him and headed out of the room and down the hall. The sound of the shower spray teased him. He shut his eyes, stifling a groan. Lilah was naked. In his bathroom. Just down the hall.

What kind of a man was he to be lusting for her body when she'd just learned about her sister's murder? A sex-starved one, he admitted to himself. There'd been no other woman he'd even thought about being with since Lilah had swept into his life that past March. She'd come home to spend time with her ill father. Her days had been spent with Chauncey, but her nights had been shared with him.

Now it was June and she'd returned pregnant. What was he to think?

Rousing from his stupor, Harlan went to his own room and stowed his gun in the chest of drawers before stripping out of his uniform. He pulled on a pair of shorts and sat on the bed, waiting for his turn in the shower. Too bad they couldn't take one together. He recalled a memorable time when they had. Her soft skin had been wet and slippery to his touch, and the needles of water had sprayed on them as they'd kissed, long and hard, hands exploring every inch of naked flesh.

Stop. Going down that particular memory lane tonight would lead to nothing but frustration and insomnia.

He didn't have to wait long for her to finish. Lilah strode past his open door and then paused. Her hair was plastered to her head, and tiny rivulets of water ran down the front of her thin tank top. Her very *reveal-*

ing top, which exposed a faint impression of nipples. His groin tightened and his heart thudded. How was he going to survive Lilah staying with him and obey her no-touch rule?

She leaned against the doorjamb, long legs crossed at the ankles and a couple inches of flat midriff exposed.

It wouldn't be flat for much longer.

Lilah slowly rubbed a towel through the ends of her long hair. "Didn't mean to act bitchy a moment ago. It's just…" She took a deep breath, and her cheeks flushed crimson. "I can't forget the way you cut me out of your life."

"Maybe I shouldn't have listened to—"

She waved an arm, dismissing his excuse. "It's done. If you cared so much about what everyone thought, then what we had wasn't as strong as I'd imagined it to be."

He rose to his feet and crossed the room. "You know my reasons. If I could do it over again, change my past decision, perhaps I would."

"Really?" Her gray eyes pierced his soul. "You might have cared about me, once—a little—but winning an election is more important to you than I ever could be. You've spent years dreaming of this opportunity. And I'd only mess it up for you."

"I won't lie. I want it bad. I want the chance to prove I'm not the kind of man my father was."

He hadn't ever revealed very much to her. Only that his dad drank too much and had been absent almost all his life. His mom had suffered a debilitating stroke last year and Harlan seemed to believe that the years of hardship she'd suffered had played a significant role in her compromised health.

"And you can't prove anything if you're associated with someone like me. A low-class Tedder. A woman with an outlaw family." Her mouth twisted. "You want some kindergarten-teaching, Sunday-school-attending, upstanding kind of gal who'll help your campaign and make you appear respectable."

He scratched the back of his neck. "When you put it like that, you make me sound like a hypocritical jerk."

A sad smile tugged at her lips. "No. I understand why winning's so important to you. I can't fault your goal to clean up the county."

The heaviness of the unspoken lay between them like a smothering blanket.

"But?" he asked, quirking a brow.

"You're the right man for the job. Everybody knows it. You have nothing to prove. And a woman like Jolene would be damn near perfect for you."

He recoiled instinctively. "I have no interest in Jolene."

Her eyes softened. "Glad to hear it. She's kind of a bitch."

The scent of soap and shampoo was all Lilah left behind as she entered her own bedroom and softly shut the door.

Harlan rubbed his face. Lilah shook him like no one else. Every word, every gesture, every touch left him broken and hungering for more. Why did he have to fall for her of all people? He lay on his bed and heard Lilah toss and turn in the next room. She should be here, lying beside him. Did she feel it, too? Need and desire tumbled within him like a summer storm.

He heard a small hiccup and bolted upright. Was she crying?

Harlan padded to the closed door and knocked. No answer. Gently, he pushed it open. Lilah lay curled with her knees drawn to her chest, knuckles stuffed in her mouth. Another moan escaped the physical barrier she'd created with her fist.

"Stop," he said gruffly, sitting beside her. The mattress gave under his weight, and her body rolled toward his. She stiffened, and he brushed a strand of damp hair that clung to her face. "Don't cry," he demanded softly. "It's not good for you or the baby."

"The baby," she sniffled. "I still can't get used to the idea."

"Are you sure it isn't mine?" he blurted.

"I'm sure," she muttered, turning her head away from him.

He leaned against the headboard and put an arm around her shoulder. A long silence stretched between them. He kissed the top of her head. "Everything's going to work out," he promised.

"I don't want to talk about it right now."

"Fine. But I'm staying here with you tonight."

Lilah pulled away and sat up. "No. You—"

He put a finger to her lips. "Shh. I just want to hold you. At least until you fall asleep."

"Promise?"

"I promise."

Slowly, she lowered her body and snuggled against

him. In almost no time, the rhythmic rise and fall of her chest assured him she'd finally fallen into a deep slumber. He stroked the side of her soft cheek, chasing away a fallen tear.

Regret twisted his gut. Had he done the right thing breaking off their relationship? Every moment he spent with her would make their goodbye so much more difficult. Still, holding her as she slept felt right. Somehow, they'd figure everything out once the immediate danger had passed.

Chapter Six

Lilah pulled her car into her uncle's driveway. If anyone had a clue what kind of new mischief Dad had gotten into before his death, Uncle Thad would know. Hell, he was probably in the thick of any criminal activity. Dad had been the master moonshine blender with the killer recipe, but Uncle Thad had the connections and a natural-born salesman's charisma.

A cloud of red dirt marked her abrupt halt at the entrance to his cabin. Holding her breath through the dust, she marched to the porch and rapped on the door.

Cousin Lavon opened it, scowling. "Since when did you start knocking?" he complained, turning his back to her and plopping down in front of the TV.

Surly guy. Poor Aunt Viola had a house full of adult children with no apparent desire to move out and get a real job.

Vi emerged from the kitchen, wiping her hands on an apron and appearing even more tired and drained than usual. Her faded olive eyes were red-tinged from crying.

"What brings you here?" she asked. "Figured you'd be

too upset about poor Darla to come a callin'. You know we'll all be at visitation tonight."

"What?" Lavon jerked his gaze away from the television. "Can't go. I got plans."

"Stop being so disrespectful." Uncle Thad strolled into the den and frowned at his eldest son. "You're going. Six o'clock sharp."

"Yes, sir," Lavon grumbled, clearly unhappy, but unwilling to disobey his father.

Uncle Thad gave her a sympathetic smile as Aunt Viola quietly slipped back into the kitchen. "Tough day for the Tedders, especially you."

Guilt flickered in her belly. She was plum tuckered from crying and had awoken this morning full of resolve to discover what might have caused her father and sister's deaths. Better that than dwelling on sorrow.

"I—I'd like to talk with you, if you have a moment." Unexpected tension twisted her tongue. Fueled by anger and despair, she hadn't thought through how best to broach the subject. And she sure hadn't counted on others being underfoot.

"Of course." He rounded on Lavon. "Leave us alone."

Lavon sprang up from the chair with just enough sass to show his displeasure, but not enough to risk his dad's anger, either.

"Vi, bring us some tea on the porch."

"I can help her with that—" Lilah began.

"No, she doesn't mind."

A little presumptuous of him deciding what his wife did and didn't mind—but what did Lilah know? They were one of the few couples in the family who'd stayed together for decades. She followed him onto the porch where he took a seat and motioned at the rocker next to him.

"What's up?"

Lilah bypassed the rocker and dragged over a chair, sitting directly across from her uncle. His gray eyes flickered at the subtle act of defiance and she suppressed a triumphant smile. Uncle Thad was one of her favorite relatives but it didn't hurt to bring him down a peg or two now and then.

Best to get straight to the point. "Have you had anyone stalk you or break into your house?"

"No." His head snapped back an inch. "You had any more trouble since the night you called me?"

"A neighbor saw a man creeping around my apartment the other night."

His brow creased. "How'd they know he targeted your apartment, specifically?"

"She caught him looking in my window and hanging out by my door."

Disgust curled his lips. "A Peeping Tom."

That hadn't occurred to her. A random coincidence? "Maybe. If there weren't two recent murders in the family, I might not even connect the two incidents."

"Still no proof that they are. The world's full of sick people."

The screen door screeched open and Aunt Vi emerged, carrying a pitcher of sweet tea and two glasses of ice. Thad pulled a silver flask from the pocket of his pants and poured a splash before angling it toward Lilah. "Care for a nip?"

She quirked a brow. He'd never offered before. "No, thanks."

"Might take the edge off your nerves. You appear mighty riled."

"No."

He shrugged and tucked it away. Behind his back, Vi nodded approvingly and slipped back into the house.

"I am shaken," she admitted, picking up her glass and taking a long, cool swallow. "I don't feel safe anywhere."

"Stay here with us. Our house is yours. Always was, always will be."

If it wasn't for the sullen Lavon, she might have been tempted. "No. You have a full house. And if someone's targeting me, I don't want to drag y'all into the mess."

"You're family," he insisted. "Couldn't bear it if something happened to you, too. You'll be safer here than anywhere else. Me, Lavon and two of the younger boys all have guns, and we won't hesitate to use them." He pulled a cigar from his front pocket and struck a lighter.

Normally, she didn't mind his porch smoking, but the scent of burning tar and tobacco had her tasting bile at the back of her throat. Quickly, she washed it down with another sip of sweet tea.

"I'm staying with Harlan Sampson for now."

The stogie almost fell out of his mouth. "Why?"

"For protection."

Uncle Thad narrowed his eyes. "You seeing that fella again?"

"No. It's just a temporary arrangement until things settle down."

"So you say."

"What's that supposed to mean?"

"You and him were hot and heavy a few months ago. I warned you then and I'll warn you now—stay away from government men. They're nothing but trouble."

Lilah started to make a crack about paranoia, then thought better of it. A little paranoia just might keep her alive at the moment. The lace curtains behind Uncle Thad moved a fraction, and she glimpsed Lavon's face at the window. The big sneak. She'd never liked him. He was a few years older than her and was always the bully at school when they were growing up.

"Harlan means well," she said stiffly, wondering how he had turned the tables on her and her decisions. She set the glass on the wicker table. "I came here to ask *you* a few questions."

His mouth puckered at the end of the cigar, and he drew a long puff of smoke, exhaling it into an elaborate chain of smoke rings. "Shoot."

"Harlan suspects you and Dad, maybe even Ed, have been business partners for more than just moonshine." She pushed through her hesitancy. "You're family, and you know I love you, but I need to ask—have y'all ever been involved in drug operations?"

Uncle Thad drew a sharp breath and coughed. "Drugs?" He coughed again and his face reddened under his beard. "I can't believe you'd ask such a thing. Insulting enough you believe me capable of such a crime—but you suspect your own father? A man who's not here to defend his reputation?"

"It's horrible, and I'm sorry. I asked because I can't explain the thirty thousand dollars cash I found hidden under his mattress."

"For all I know, Chauncey had been saving that money for years. Not really all that much for a lifetime of savings, if you ask me."

"So you deny branching out into marijuana and heavier stuff?"

"I won't even dignify that with an answer." He took a long swallow of 'shine-laced tea.

Awful early for indulging. She'd never observed him to be a heavy drinker, unlike her dad, but the recent deaths apparently weighed as heavy on his heart as they did on her own. Still, she had to push.

"I only ask because there's some reason for the killings."

"I loved Chauncey, but my brother was a hothead. He got in a rousing bar fight at least once or twice a month. You ask me, someone came up there to his cabin to settle a grudge."

"Maybe. But what about Darla? How do you explain that?"

His face darkened and his left hand balled into a fist. "Word is—the cops think it's Ed."

"You can't believe that. He loved her. I was with him when he had to identify Darla's body. The poor guy fell apart."

"Guilt can do that to a man."

"Grief, not guilt." Was she the only one who believed

him innocent? "Thought you liked Ed—wasn't he working with you and Dad on the side for extra money?"

Uncle Thad drew another long puff of tobacco. A shuttered expression on his face replaced the simmering anger. Lilah remembered that look well. He and Dad wore it often when someone inquired too closely about their business.

"He didn't do much outside of a few deliveries," Thad grumbled.

"At a significant risk. Sounds like Ed was the one risking the rap for distribution."

He ignored the subtle gibe. "You know it's usually a spouse in these kinds of cases, don't you? Crimes of passion happen all the time."

Lilah set down her glass with an emphatic thud. "You used to preach family loyalty."

"Ed Stovall is an outsider."

"How can you say that? He was married to Darla for years. They have three children."

"He only married her 'cause Chauncey forced the issue."

"It may have started that way, but they stayed together. That should count for something."

Hearing a crunch of tires on gravel, Lilah turned her head and spotted the familiar brown-and-white cruiser pulling in. She groaned inwardly. What was Harlan doing way out here? Checking up on her? She shouldn't have left a note in the kitchen telling him where she was going. Any hope of gaining information from Uncle Thad was lost for the time being.

The car stopped and he exited, his long and slender

frame slowly unfolding in the sun's glare. He stared at them from behind dark polarized sunglasses, but she knew by the twitch of a muscle in his jaw that he was seriously annoyed.

Too bad. So was she.

WHAT GOOD WAS it to have Lilah stay at his house for protection if she ran around all over these mountains without an escort?

Not a damn bit.

Harlan slammed the car door and made his way to the porch, working to control his irritation. It's not as if he'd spelled out the danger to Lilah, but surely she had enough sense to realize she'd put herself in a vulnerable position.

Time to be clearer.

With an effort, he twisted his mouth into a humorless smile, climbed the porch steps and extended a hand to Thaddeus Tedder. "Morning."

Thad rose, obvious reluctance in the slow extension of his own hand. "Harlan."

Lilah smiled brightly. "So you got my note. Want a glass of sweet tea?"

She wore a pink sundress and her loose blond waves tumbled about her shoulders. For all the world, she appeared carefree and poised. But he'd held her last night as she'd cried for her sister, and the faint smudge of purple under her eyes belied the strain she'd been under. A strain for which he was partly responsible.

"No, thanks. I'll pass on the tea," he replied.

Thad gestured to a chair. "Lilah tells me she's staying with you for a spell."

He sat down, aware that Thaddeus was far from pleased at the news. "Seemed for the best."

"She can stay with me. It don't look good—her staying at yer place."

He glanced at Lilah. Spots of red dotted her cheeks. What did her uncle know about them? If he wasn't aware of their prior relationship, he would be in a few weeks. Everyone would be. And they were bound to think he was the one who got her pregnant. And perhaps he was.

"Nobody cares these days," she quickly chimed in. "It's only temporary, anyway."

"Ask me, you should put a ring on that girl's finger. Now that Chauncey's passed away, it's my duty to look after her welfare."

Lilah stood and dug her car keys out of her purse. "It's my decision and no one else's." She went to the screen door and called, "Thanks for the tea, Aunt Vi. Catch you later."

Hastily, Harlan said goodbye to Thad and followed Lilah down the porch steps to her car. Even with his long loping strides, he had to hurry to catch up to her.

"We need to talk," he said as she opened the car door.

"Not now. Not here. Shouldn't you be out arresting bad guys or something?"

"Protecting you is part of my job."

"I'm fine. Nothing's going to happen to me in the middle of the day."

She slid in and closed the door, but Harlan leaned in the open window. "Darla was shot in broad daylight."

Lilah flinched and he wanted to kick himself. He opened his mouth to apologize, then snapped it shut. The reminder was for her own good.

"She was alone at her house," Lilah replied. "I'm here with family. There's a difference."

"No one is above suspicion."

Pfft. "Warning received." Lilah inserted the key and turned the motor over.

This wouldn't do. He didn't want to leave her angry and upset. "Wait a sec. I came home for lunch but never ate. Let's call a truce. Want to grab a bite with me?"

Her hand hovered over the ignition. "I *am* hungry," she admitted, a sheepish smile curving her lips.

"Lucille's Barbecue?" It was her favorite. She couldn't say no to that.

"Deal."

He opened her door and gestured at the cruiser. "Come with me. We'll swing by after and pick up your car."

Twenty minutes later, he congratulated himself. Good call on taking her to lunch. Lucille's was bustling with the clatter of plates and silverware and chattering patrons as they placed their order, and an enticing aroma of smoked pork wafted through the country diner. It was plain with red-topped Formica tables and scuffed aluminum chairs, but the barbecue was the best in three counties.

He quirked a brow at Lilah as the waitress walked away, scribbling down their order. "A salad? Who are you?"

"Figured I needed to clean up my act a little for the next few months."

Her smile was thin, and he was struck at how delicate she appeared, how frail. Life had dealt her nothing but hard blows lately.

Elbert Anders and his two brothers approached— mouths and shoulders sloped downward, but their eyes were determined and lit with commiseration. Elbert came to a standstill by their table and his brothers aligned on either side of his large, bulky frame. The mountain men all sported long bushy beards and wore faded denim overalls. Privately, Harlan dubbed them the ZZ Top triplets. "Sorry 'bout Darla," Elbert mumbled. "We'll be payin' our respects tonight."

"Thank you," Lilah whispered.

It was as if Elbert had opened an invisible barrier between them and the diner patrons. Slowly, others drifted over and expressed their condolences. Tedder or not, the folks around here felt sorry for Lilah losing her father and now her sister. Harlan's spine stiffened as J.D. rose from the back and sauntered their way.

"Sorry for your loss," he said to Lilah, slipping Harlan a loaded look.

Her mouth compressed in a thin line, and she gave a stiff nod, turning her chin away a fraction. A subtle rejection.

"Our office is working tirelessly to find the person responsible for Darla's murder."

"Like you did for Dad?"

"It's an open investigation. We'll get to the bottom of it."

"By harassing my brother-in-law?"

J.D. shot him a can't-you-control-your-woman look,

and Harlan laid a hand over Lilah's, stifling her drumming fingers. "We have to explore all avenues," he said quietly.

The waitress glided over with a tray and set down their orders. "Eat up, darlin'," she urged Lilah, patting her shoulder. "You lookin' mighty frail."

Lilah flashed a real smile at the waitress and J.D. ambled out the door, pausing at a few tables to shake hands. Ever the politician—an aspect of running for sheriff that Harlan despised. Genuine interest in others was fine, but continual grandstanding was another. But who was he to judge? He'd sacrificed a relationship for the sake of the upcoming election.

"She's right," said Harlan. "You need to eat up. Want a bite of my barbecue sandwich?"

Lilah shook her head and poured dressing over her salad. "Not really all that hungry anymore."

"But—"

"I know. I'm eating for two." She dug into her salad with determination.

"I'll be with you tonight. You won't be by yourself at the viewing."

"I still have family left," she pointed out. "I'm not completely alone."

"Of course," he quickly agreed, realizing he'd been put in his place. "I just don't want you to be out and about without me until we catch this killer."

"Let's get this straight between us right now. I'm only staying with you temporarily. I'm not without resources. We're just friends."

Friends. Ouch.

She jabbed a tomato with her fork. "And you don't have the right to tell me what to do. Especially not after the way you broke things off with me. Got it?"

"Message received loud and clear. Now eat," he commanded.

Her face flushed and thunder gathered in her eyes.

"Um…please?" he mumbled.

"That's better."

Swiftly, he changed topics. "Spoke with the medical examiner today. Darla's personal effects at the time of death only included clothes and shoes. No jewelry."

"Not even her wedding ring?"

"No."

"Could somebody have killed her just for her wedding ring?"

"Unlikely. Seems to me as if the killer wanted to disassociate any connection with Darla. It's personal."

"You mean Ed," she said flatly. "Still not buying it. Aren't crimes of passion committed in the heat of the moment? My sister was shot in the back in her own yard. No face-to-face spur-of-the-moment killing there. Just like it wasn't with Dad."

"I'm not saying your theory about a drug deal gone bad isn't possible. But we have no proof that your family's been involved in that."

"What else could it possibly be?"

"That's what we're trying to find out." He thought of the failed drug raids. The worm of suspicion still wiggled beneath the surface of his mind. Drug operations gone bad were notoriously bloody, and yet there was nothing to tie the murders to that theory. Still, he couldn't discount the drug angle.

But why would anyone stalk Lilah at her apartment? She lived away from Lavender Mountain and had no immediate connection to anyone involved in illegal activities, anymore. Well, she did still have extended family, a couple of uncles and a number of cousins.

Unless the stalking was an isolated incident. A coincidence.

Thing is, he didn't believe in coincidences.

Chapter Seven

Lilah hated funeral homes. Hated the cloying scent of lilies, the whispered conversations, the piped organ music and the people stiffly dressed in their Sunday clothes. And she especially hated open caskets for viewing. She kept her face averted from the front of the room where family and friends paid their last respects. Tomorrow, she would go out to Dad's old cabin, toss daisies into the wind and say her own private goodbyes. Her eyes slid to the clock mounted on the sidewall. A few minutes past the hour. Soon, everyone but Ed and his parents and kids would be gone, and then she could slip out as well.

Ed's parents herded the children down the aisle and Lilah rose to say goodbye. A few more people left the room, until it was only she and Harlan in the pew area and Ed speaking with the funeral home director.

A loud voice erupted from the back corner of the room, and she turned around.

Uncle Thad and Uncle Jasper were having words— heated words, judging by the flush of color on their cheeks and the tense set of their jaws. Her reclusive Uncle Jasper didn't get along well with others. Never had. But an argument now was totally inappropriate. She started toward them, motioning Harlan not to follow, but Uncle Thad beat a hasty exit without a backward glance.

"What was that all about?" she asked Jasper.

He swallowed hard, Adam's apple bobbling up and down his scrawny neck. "Sorry for the unseemly behavior," he said in his reedy formal voice. He pulled at his tie. "How you holding up, LayLay?"

His use of her childhood nickname nearly undid her. "Making it," she responded gruffly. "You and Uncle Thad having words?"

"That's nothing new. Reason why I prefer to keep to myself. Life's easier alone."

"Don't you ever get lonely?" She didn't understand his hermit-like existence. Jasper had never married, had no friends and seemingly no need for much contact with the outside world. He lived alone at the top of Widow's Peak Mountain in a primitive cabin and kept a garden. His wants seemed few and simple.

"Lonely?" He rubbed his chin. "Nah, I'm used to solitude."

"You're doing okay?" she asked uncertainly. They'd never been close—Uncle Jasper didn't allow others to get too close—but his gruff manner had never insulted her. When she'd been a child, he'd once made her a doll fashioned from straw, and she'd appreciated the gesture, even if he'd shoved it in her hands with no comment.

Gray-blue eyes narrowed on his wrinkled face. "Why? You sayin' I look unseemly?"

"No, no," she said hastily. "It's just… You're getting

older. I worry something might happen to you all alone up there."

"The Good Lord will take me when he sees fit. You're the one who needs to be careful." His gaze shifted to Darla's casket. "Bad things happening all over again."

Her heart quickened. "Again?"

"There's bad blood in this family, goin' way back. It's poisoned all our lives."

"What do you mean? That we've been unlucky in our share of tragedy?"

He pinned her with a hard stare. "Doomed."

"You're being superstitious," she said, ignoring the goose bumps climbing up her arms. Bad enough spending hours in a room with her sister's body without listening to her uncle's old-fashioned ideas about family curses. Nervously, she fiddled with the leather bracelet on her left wrist. Its crimson stone glittered like a droplet of blood. "There's a reason for Dad and Darla's murders. The police are working on it."

"Tedders ain't got no business cottoning to the police."

Jasper had never been in the moonshine business with the rest of the family, but he evidently still shared their contempt of the law.

"We have to cooperate with them." She drew a deep, steadying breath. "Do you know if Dad and Uncle Thad might have gotten into something dangerous? Like drugs?"

"There's worse things than moonshine and drugs, like a poisoned history. There's a reason I'm so scarred and a hermit. A reason yer dad was an alcoholic and Thad so…controlling. Go away. Move away from the mountain and never come back."

"Not until I find out who's responsible for all this." She owed her family that much. And if someone was after her, she had to discover the killer to save her baby.

He nodded his head at something over her shoulder. "That there yer fella?"

She glanced back to find Harlan ambling his way toward them.

"He's a friend. Now, tell me, what were you and Uncle Thad arguing about?" she asked once more, hoping he'd open up before Harlan arrived at her side.

"Don't never be alone with Thaddeus," he warned, his lowered voice urgent and intense. "He's dangerous. He and that boy of his, Lavon, ain't to be trusted."

Dangerous? Uncle Thad was a staple in her life. Warm, kind and always generous when money had been short growing up. "Lavon's a bully, but Uncle Thad's no danger. What are you implying?"

But Jasper clamped his thin lips together and stared mutinously at Harlan who'd stepped up beside her.

"Evening, Jasper," Harlan said, holding out his hand.

Uncle Jasper pointedly ignored the proffered handshake. Harlan shrugged and dropped his arm.

Without a word, Jasper turned his back and headed to the door.

"Wait," she called after him. "I'd like to come visit if that's okay. We need to talk more."

Jasper didn't bother facing them as he answered. "I've said all I have to say on the matter."

"Charming as usual," Harlan commented drily. "What's going on?"

She shook her head. "He gets stranger every year. Kept going on about our family being doomed and poisoned."

"Anything else?"

Lilah hesitated. It felt disloyal to repeat what he'd said about Uncle Thad and Lavon. "That's mostly everything. I need to pay him a visit."

"No. You need to stay put at my house until we've uncovered who's responsible for the murders."

"But—"

"No *buts*. It's too dangerous. If you won't think of yourself, think of your baby."

His words vibrated warm and deep in her core. Even though she'd told him it wasn't his, Harlan still cared about her unborn child. If she wasn't careful, she could lose her heart to him all over again. Lilah lifted her chin.

"I *am* thinking of the baby. We need to solve these crimes. Fast."

"No. *I* need to solve them. You stay out of it. I'm working on it. Trust me." He guided her by the elbow toward the door. "Let's talk about it outside. We'll catch Ed when he's finished his business with the funeral home."

She pushed through the large wooden door. "Sounds to me like the sheriff's office is only out to railroad poor Ed. As for Dad, you've suggested it's probably nothing more than a riled customer or someone he fought with in a bar."

"We're looking at the possible drug angle as well,"

he said defensively. "Although, every lead seems to turn into a dead end."

Lilah slipped out the door into the night's darkness. A full moon shone, lime green and mysterious. She inhaled the fresh air and hugged her arms over her chest. "I hope you didn't come with me tonight just to try and corner Ed after the visitation and question him about dealing drugs. He's been through the wringer the past few days. Leave him be."

Harlan shook his head. "The man gets a pass tonight. I'm not heartless."

Heartless Harlan. Lilah felt a sad smile tug the edges of her mouth. After what he'd put her through these past few weeks, she'd say the moniker fit. But what he lacked in heart, he made up for with his dogged determination to do the right thing. She would give him that much. Another woman might be satisfied with those crumbs, but she wasn't. Not by a long shot.

"Speaking of being through the wringer, you look pale. You sure you're okay?" he asked, frowning down at her.

"I won't lie, it's been tough," she admitted. "What happened to Dad was horrible, but he was living his last days, dying from cirrhosis. But Darla is…" She stumbled on the words. "Darla was only a few years older than me. And she has left behind three small children."

"I'm going to get to the bottom of this." His voice was gentle but laced with steel. "I promise you that."

A whoosh of stale air, and Ed emerged from the funeral home, shoulders sagging and head down.

"Need a lift home?" Harlan asked.

Ed jerked his head up. "What?" He swiped at his cheeks and coughed. "Oh, no. Thanks. I'm fine."

Lilah's heart pinched at the sight of his grief. She embraced him in a quick hug, but not so brief that she didn't catch the sharp, sour scent of liquor on his breath. Her worry increased. A few drinks to get through this horrid week was one thing, but if this led to an addiction, she feared for her nephews. Those kids needed him sober.

"So sorry, Ed," she said past the catch in her throat.

Harlan's mouth tightened. "You been drinking, by any chance? If so, I'm going to have to insist on driving you home."

"Just a couple before visitation started," he protested, running a hand through his long thick hair. "Unfortunately, the buzz has entirely worn off."

"Walk a straight line for me."

Ed rolled his eyes but obeyed. His large body didn't sway in the least. He walked back to them and then lifted his right knee and balanced easily. "There. I know the cop's whole repertoire. You want to take me to the station and make me take a Breathalyzer test, go ahead."

"That won't be necessary."

Lilah shot Harlan a dark look before turning to Ed. "This might not be the right time to bring this up, but I wanted you to know…" She hesitated. How to bring this up delicately? "If you need any help with funeral expenses, I talked to Jimmy and we'll both chip in what we can."

Ed stuck his hands in his pockets. "That's awful generous, 'specially considering the way we helped ourselves to the money you found in your dad's cabin."

"Forget about it," she said hastily. If only she could erase the memory of her last talk—no argument, call it what it really was—with her sister over the damned money. That was something she'd have to live with the rest of her life.

"That money will more than cover the burial costs. I returned the new truck and cancelled the kitchen makeover."

What a relief her brother-in-law had a sensible head on his shoulders after all. "That sounds like a good plan. Still, I'm here. If you need help with the kids, well, with anything, let me know."

"Did you ever find Darla's wedding ring?" Harlan asked suddenly.

Again, she shot him a warning look. "Really, now's not the time for you—"

"No. Never did," Ed interrupted. "I searched everywhere, too." His sad brown eyes sought hers. "Couldn't even find that new stuff you discovered at your dad's, Lilah. Hope they weren't some kind of family heirlooms."

"Was she wearing the found pieces last time you saw her?" Harlan asked.

The man couldn't seem to help himself when it came to asking questions. She frowned at him.

Ed's brow furrowed. "Might have been. Can't rightly recall."

"It's no big deal," she assured Ed. "Don't you give it another thought. They weren't valuable, and none of us knew where they came from." She held up her right wrist. "And I have this. Darla insisted I keep one of the pieces."

"Good." He shuffled his feet and stole a glance at Harlan. "Guess I'll be moseying on home now, if you don't mind. I'm beat."

"You be careful," she said softly, awkwardly patting his shoulder.

They watched as he climbed into his old truck and drove off.

"Maybe you should tell me more about this jewelry," Harlan said slowly.

She cocked her head to the side. "Like I told Ed, they weren't valuable at all. Just costume jewelry."

"Humor me."

"This bracelet, a cameo ring and a glass beaded neck-lace."

He took her hand in his and examined the bracelet. The red stone glittered under the moonbeams.

"Told you. Nothing special."

He didn't speak anymore as they got in his cruiser and drove the twisted roads up Lavender Mountain to his place. Lilah laid her head against the cool pane of glass on the passenger side, mind swimming with images of the people who'd come to say their last good-byes to Darla.

Let this be the end. No more deaths. No more gut-wrenching phone calls, funerals or heartache.

At Harlan's, they silently entered and switched on the lights. What she needed was a nice long shower. In his bathroom, she stripped and stepped into the shower's hot spray. She reached for the shelf that held soap and shampoo and discovered a familiar bottle of pink gardenia bath gel. Her fingers curled around it as a silly grin split her face. *Her* shower gel that she'd left there in March.

Why hadn't Harlan thrown it away? Had he hoped she would return one day? Maybe she was reading too much into it, but the possibility lifted her heart for a moment.

Cleaned and refreshed, Lilah went to bed and slipped under the fresh sheets, waiting on the welcome absolution of sleep.

HER LEGS TWISTED in the bedsheets and she fought for air. Something deep, dark and heavy pressed on her chest as an unknown menace approached that was familiar but suddenly ominous. It slithered toward her paralyzed body, coiled to strike.

"Lilah, Lilah. Baby, you're safe. I'm here."

Her cramped lungs released and she sucked in oxygen. Harlan's hand splayed over her left breast, calming her pounding heart.

"Shh," he murmured. "Go back to sleep."

She sighed and took comfort in his body stretched out behind her. Despite everything, despite her anger and hurt and her best intentions to keep her pride intact…in the night, Harlan was the one she reached for, the man she wanted beside her. She rubbed her face against the hard muscled biceps wrapped around her. Tonight, she wouldn't fight it. Lilah closed her eyes and sank into dreamless oblivion.

Chapter Eight

"I need the file on the old Hilltop Strangler case," Harlan said.

Zelda, a middle-aged administrative staple in the sheriff's office, and near as powerful as J.D., looked up from the payroll spreadsheet numbers she'd been inputting on the computer. She lowered her tortoiseshell bifocals and stared. "That so? Nobody's looked at that in ages. Not that I know of, anyway."

"Doesn't hurt to take a peek at it occasionally," he said noncommittally. No need to get folks stirred up on a wild-goose chase. This quick glance was only a way to satisfy his overactive imagination.

"So you say." Her intelligent gray eyes sharpened but she rose and went to the row of old steel file cabinets. In seconds, she produced a thick manila envelope bulging with yellowed papers.

"Got to appreciate a man who wants to look at the real paperwork and not the scanned reports," she said with a nod.

"Call me old-fashioned." The computer was a huge convenience, but sometimes all the documents weren't scanned and the photographic detail was often blurred. He preferred to study the original black-and-white photos.

He tucked the folder under an arm. "Thanks."

"How's your girlfriend doing?" she asked, amusement spiking her eyes.

Harlan inwardly groaned. She was as bad as the guys. Ever since Lilah's oh-so-public announcement of her pregnancy, the teasing had been unmerciful. Everyone kept pressing him, curious if the baby might really be his after all.

"She's fine," he answered tersely, cutting off the discussion.

Zelda smirked. "Don't forget to invite me to the baby shower."

He beat a hasty retreat back to his office and opened the file, spreading its contents over his desk. The original police reports were typewritten and riddled with smattering blotches of white correction fluid. No convenient delete key twenty-five years ago when these reports were made. He opened the tattered envelope of photographs.

Victim number one, Amzie Billbray. Age thirty-two, white female.

Victim number two, Raylene Rucker. Age twenty-eight, white female.

Both females were described as a "fallen woman"—a polite euphemism back then for a prostitute. Each looked at least a decade older than her real age—gaunt mountain women with bleak eyes and thin joyless lips that tugged down in the corners. No amount of dark lipstick or blush could completely cover that veneer of desperation.

There appeared to be nothing in common between the victims, other than their shared profession. Both of them were strangled after sexual contact. Both of them were found with their faces buried in their pillows. Despite an intense investigation, no one was ever charged. The only clue was that the victims' friends claimed each of the women was wearing a piece of jewelry that was never found. Cheap costume baubles, they'd insisted, certainly nothing valuable or that would lure a robber to attack them.

Still, the police took notice, believing the murderer might have taken the items as trophies. Mementos whereby the killer felt linked to the women he'd killed and took secret pleasure in reliving his violent crime.

The two killings were a few months apart, and then—inexplicably—no more victims were ever found. It was as if the killer had either spent all his rage (highly unlikely), had moved away, gone to jail, or had died.

Harlan flipped through the dozens of photos, most of them of the crime scenes, until he found the one he sought.

One of Raylene's cousins had provided police with a picture of her wearing the missing bracelet. The photographer had cropped the image to Raylene's wrist and had enlarged the photo.

Harlan squinted at it. It was a leather braided bracelet with two small copper discs alongside a small stone. He flipped the photo over and read the handwriting:

"brown leather with a garnet chip and two copper discs engraved with the initials *RR*."

His chest squeezed and his fingers went numb. *No.* What were the chances? Had Lilah really found one of the missing pieces to the old killings? Excitement warred with fear for her safety. But if that *was* Raylene's bracelet, then more than likely Chauncey Tedder had been the murderer all along. And he was now dead.

Harlan leaned back in the chair and steepled his fingers, reasoning out the implications. It wasn't as if he'd been close to Lilah's dad, but he'd always rather liked Chauncey. Sure, he'd been a hotheaded ole cuss when drunk, and he'd been involved in making illegal 'shine, but Chauncey had seemed a decent sort of man for all that. Hard to wrap his mind around Chauncey strangling two women.

If it were true, the news would tear Lilah up inside. Damn, she'd been through enough and was pregnant on top of it all. He hoped to God that when he examined her bracelet tonight it wouldn't have those engraved discs. Quickly, he scanned the rest of the report until he found a written description of the other two missing pieces, a glass beaded necklace and a cameo ring. He picked up that page and the bracelet picture to make photocopies to show Lilah.

"What ya up to?"

J.D. strolled into the room and sank his considerable girth into the chair in front of Harlan's desk. Beefy fingers pawed at the old reports.

Of course, Zelda had told him he'd checked out the file. That woman knew where her bread was buttered.

"Just looking over this old case," said Harlan.

"Any particular reason?"

J.D.'s hands fumbled at the pocket of his shirt uniform, then dropped by his side. The sheriff had given
up smoking years ago, but still reached for a phantom
cigarette when he wanted to settle in for a chat.

"No," Harlan lied. He needed to get his facts straight
first and then break the bad news to Lilah if Chauncey
ended up being a postmortem suspect. No way he'd let
her hear this news secondhand.

"So out of the blue, you decided to comb through it this
afternoon? Strange. No one's requested that file in years."

"Keep up with it, do you?"

J.D. shrugged his massive shoulders. "Glanced at
the checkout record Zelda keeps when she told me you
wanted to review those old murders. Not like you've
shown much interest until now. Doubt the murders cross
anyone's radars these days. So, naturally, this makes
me wonder if there's a reason for your sudden interest."

Harlan supposed that curiosity was a deeply ingrained personality trait in law enforcement work, but
J.D.'s questioning made him slightly uncomfortable and
defensive. Their professional relationship had cooled
since Lilah had returned to Lavender Mountain.

"You should be glad when employees keep up with
these old cases."

"Never hurts, never hurts," J.D. mumbled. "Anything
new going on?"

"Nope. Same old stuff."

"That Tedder girl got you on your toes? We don't see
much of you at Hazel's bar these days."

"Her name's Lilah, and I've been busy, that's all."

"Sure you have." J.D. rose and lumbered to the door. He paused in the doorway. "Just 'cause she got knocked up is no reason to flush your career down the toilet. If a paternity test shows you're the father, agree to pay child support and move on. I think the good citizens of this county would raise their brows at you marrying a Tedder."

Anger sparked up and down his spine, and he rose. "The good citizens of this county can kiss my ass, then."

J.D. sadly shook his head. "See what happens when you lie in bed with a Tedder? Problems. Sometimes you're better off letting sleeping dogs lie." With that parting quip, he disappeared down the hallway.

That was a hell of an attitude for the county's chief law enforcement officer to espouse.

Harlan slapped the Hilltop Strangler paperwork back in the folder, except for the photo and the missing jewelry description. The case might be old, but it was far from cold.

Despite his simmering anger, J.D. did have a point. If Chauncey turned out to be a serial killer, any affiliation with a Tedder would be a death knell on his dream of becoming sheriff. And this county needed him. J.D. had gotten old and lazy and had let things slide.

Harlan only hoped it wasn't too late to turn back crime in Elmore County.

LILAH PULLED THE biscuits out of the oven and inhaled the fresh-bread aroma. No telling what time Harlan would return; his hours were erratic. She'd go ahead and treat

herself to a biscuit. She slathered its golden top with butter and groaned with pleasure as she bit into the home-
baked goodness. Too bad Harlan didn't keep cans of
preserves. She could buy some apples and peaches tomorrow and spend the day canning.

Abruptly, she lowered the biscuit and grimaced. *Don't
get too comfy and domesticated here.* This living arrangement was temporary, best to keep that in mind.

The door opened and a familiar set of footsteps
sounded from the den.

"Smells good in here." Harlan entered the kitchen
and flashed a wan smile.

"What's wrong?"

He dropped the smile. "Am I that obvious?"

"No, but I can read you."

"That's scary," he tried to joke. "It can wait until
after dinner."

"Uh-uh, I'll just worry. Tell me now."

"It might not be anything." He came to her side and
the usual tingle ran down her skin at his nearness, but
instead of embracing her, Harlan lifted her right wrist
and twisted the leather band of her bracelet.

"What are you doing?"

"Take it off."

She shrugged. "Okay. You sure are acting weird. It's
just something I found—"

"—in your dad's cabin. I remember."

He unhooked the clasp and held the strip of leather
up to the overhead light. "Damn it!"

Dread clawed at her gut. "What?"

Lines grooved in his forehead and his eyes were shadowed with pity as he faced her.

"I'm not going to like this news, am I?" asked Lilah.

"Sit down."

He scraped back a kitchen chair and she perched on the edge of the wooden seat, clasping her hands in her lap.

Ping. Her cell phone chirruped from the counter. *Ping.*

Might as well answer. It could be important. Lilah grabbed it and clicked open the text messenger.

Hey, there…everything ok? Where ya been? Miss seeing u 'round here. When are u coming back? Luke.

Should have known. Nice guy, but a pest. She sighed and tossed the phone on the kitchen table.

"Who was it?"

"Luke." His jaw tightened.

"You met him at my apartment complex the morning—" she swallowed "—that Darla died and you came to tell me."

"What does he want?"

Lilah lifted her shoulders. "Said he wondered how I was and why I haven't been home."

"You sure he's only a friend?" he asked, a sharp edge in his voice.

She squirmed and then straightened her back. "We saw each other for a bit after you stopped calling me."

He opened his mouth, no doubt to ask if Luke was

the one who had gotten her pregnant. She rushed to cut him off. "Tell me about the bracelet."

Harlan nodded and pointed to the back of one of the copper disks. "Can you see that? It's engraved with the initials *RR*."

She squinted at the corroded copper and the initials showed faintly. "Okay. Who's this *RR* person?"

"Raylene Rucker. The original owner."

Raylene...the name tickled the far recesses of her memory but she couldn't quite recall where she'd heard it before.

"She was murdered twenty-five years ago along with another woman, Amzie Billbray."

Images flooded her brain—newspaper headlines of the Hilltop Strangler and whispered conversations from her childhood. Lilah scooted back her chair, as if trying to distance herself from any connection so foul. The scrape of chair and tile was as loud as a gunshot. How could such a small strip of leather create such terror? She felt dizzy. Unmoored.

"How... What...?"

"When you told me about the jewelry last night, it rang a bell. Especially since you'd also found such a large cache of hidden money. That, coupled with the fact that your sister's wedding ring and the other two pieces you found also went missing, well, it all added up to a mystery."

He clasped her hands in his and it grounded her swirling emotions.

"I asked myself if there were any patterns to a past crime and realized there were. So..." He released his hands and pulled a couple of slips of paper from his pant pockets. "Take a look."

With trembling hands, she took the papers and looked down. There. Her—no Raylene's—bracelet in black-and-white with the unmistakable damnable engraving. "I can't believe it."

"Read the description of the other two items. Do they also match what you found and gave Darla?"

"A silver cameo ring and a necklace of colored glass beads. Yes."

The paper slipped from her numbed hands and fluttered to the floor like a dead thing. "I don't understand," she whispered.

"We'll get to the bottom of it," he assured her.

Did she want him to? Lilah stood abruptly and began pacing the small kitchen. "Someone put them there," she mumbled, thinking aloud. "That's why an intruder broke into the cabin and stalked me at my apartment. They were looking for them." She whirled and faced Harlan. "Why? Nobody's going to recognize that stuff after all these years. They're in no danger."

"Some killers like to keep a physical connection to their victims, to the memory of the crime."

"That's disgusting." She sat back down and twisted a lock of hair. "And what were they doing in Dad's cabin? Was he hiding them for someone?"

"Could be," Harlan said flatly.

"Why would he do such a thing? I don't get it."

"Unless the killer was someone very close to him. Someone he loved."

"He wasn't all that close to anyone. After Mom left,

he became almost as reclusive as Jasper. Never dated, never went out much."

"He still had family. Brothers, cousins, in-laws. Maybe he was covering for one of them."

She shook her head. "I can't see it."

"There's another alternative," he said slowly.

Lilah stared at him, puzzled. "Like maybe the killer saw the abandoned cabin and thought it would be safe to store the jewelry there? But he could've kept them wherever they'd been all this time. No one had ever discovered his hiding place before."

"A highly unlikely scenario. Besides, the killer would want to keep his trophies close by."

She drummed her fingers on the kitchen table. "The killer could have put it there to frame my dad for the murders."

"He have any enemies you know of?"

"Not really. He got in plenty of bar fights but those drunken brawls always seemed to blow over."

"There's other scenarios here."

She tapped an index finger to her lips. "Could be the killer wanted to buy a pint of moonshine and didn't have cash. So he gave the jewelry to Dad as collateral and intended to return on payday."

"No. Highly unlikely. I still say the killer wouldn't have parted with the trophies for any length of time."

"Maybe the moonshine buyer stole the jewelry from the killer."

"If you're going to steal, you'd pick an item a lot more valuable than a handful of costume jewelry."

She threw up her hands. "What's your theory?"

"There's another option you haven't considered." His voice was soft but pregnant with meaning. Blistering eyes pierced through her fog of confusion.

"If you mean what I think you mean, then you're one hundred percent wrong!" She jumped up so fast, her chair crashed to the floor.

"Calm down." Harlan righted the chair and guided her back into it. "At least consider the possibility."

"My dad wouldn't have killed anyone! How could you think that? You...you bastard!"

He regarded her impassively. "I'm a cop. If I see physical evidence, I have to at least consider the obvious conclusion."

"Damn your logic. You knew my dad. He wasn't a murderer." Anger sparked in every synapse of her brain and body. How dare Harlan suggest such a thing!

"Lilah, be reasonable. If you were in my shoes, you'd draw the same conclusion. At least keep an open mind and—"

"No! And don't tell me to calm down." Lord, she hated to be told that. Made her ten times as angry.

"It's not good for you or—"

"Oh, shut up," she snapped. "What if I accused your father or mother of murder? How would you feel?"

"Maybe you wouldn't be so far off the mark," he said enigmatically. His eyes darkened to the blue-blackness of a storm at sea.

"Don't turn this around on me and play your mind games."

"I'm not into playing games. I'm dead serious."

She couldn't deal with a new set of revelations. Not

now. Lilah covered her face with her hands, her entire body trembling with shock.

Harlan stroked her scalp and it felt so good, so comforting. But no, he couldn't fling wild accusations and expect his touch to bring her around like a stray dog needy for scraps of affection. She removed her hands from her face.

"Dad was *not* a murderer. I don't care if he's the convenient answer for you. Dig deeper."

"Of course we will. I'm only trying to prepare you for what's to come."

"Who all knows about this?"

"Just the two of us."

"Can we keep it that way?" The moment she asked, Lilah realized the futility of asking Harlan to suppress evidence. She couldn't ask him to jeopardize his career or compromise his principles. "Never mind."

"I am sorry. I'll speak to J.D. first thing in the morning. Maybe we can keep this matter from going public."

A bitter laugh escaped her throat. "No. It'll leak, eventually. And Dad's not here to defend himself. The Tedder name was always mud in these parts, but there's a world of difference between peddling moonshine and murdering prostitutes."

"Your true friends will stand by you."

"I don't have any friends on Lavender Mountain. Between Dad's fighting and liquor business and Darla's promiscuous high school days, I was always looked down on."

"I never realized it was a problem for you. Jimmy always seemed to get on well enough."

"My brother would beat the crap out of anyone who spoke ill of us. It's different for a girl."

He scratched his chin. "Does it really matter what anyone thinks?"

"You're a fine one to say that. You broke up with me because of my family's reputation." And now, *this*. Damn, he must be ready to ditch her once and for all. "Bet you're going to catch hell from J.D. when he hears the latest. He'll demand you kick me out of your house at once. How do you expect to win an election if you live with the woman the townsfolk will call the Hilltop Strangler's daughter?"

"You let me worry about that."

He was right. She had enough on her plate. Wearily, she rose and stumbled toward the hallway.

"Where are you going?" he called after her.

"To bed."

"Without dinner?"

"Not hungry. Besides, I'm still angry. You know my dad didn't do this."

It seemed a mile to her bedroom and she trudged along with leaden legs. Lethargy swept over her body in waves. At last, she reached the bedroom, lay down in the darkness and curled into herself. All she wanted was the blessed oblivion of sleep.

Dad couldn't have murdered those two women. She'd never seen him lay a hand on Mom, even when they were in the midst of their worst screaming matches. There had to be some reasonable explanation as to why that jewelry had been hidden under his mattress. Chauncey Tedder was not a killer.

Or was he?

She banished the disturbing question, refusing to entertain her mind's dark whisperings.

Chapter Nine

"And that's why I looked at the old Hilltop Strangler case yesterday," Harlan said, shoving the leather bracelet across J.D.'s desk.

The sheriff peered at it through the plastic zip bag in which Harlan had encased it. His, Lilah's and Darla's fingerprints were all over the thing, but maybe the forensic techs could find a useful clue anyway.

"I'll mail it to the lab in Atlanta and have them take a look. With any luck, Chauncey's prints will be on there. Old coot must have been guilty."

"Probably," Harlan admitted. "Guess you'll want a statement from Lilah on where and when she found it? Maybe talk to Chauncey's ex?"

"Sure thing. And don't you worry, I'll do you a favor and keep this whole affair low key. Forensics has a huge backlog. It'll take weeks before they examine the bracelet. We'll wrap up the case after the election in a couple months and announce to the press that the murders have been solved."

J.D.'s casual dismissal of Elmore County's most notorious unsolved crimes caught Harlan off-guard.

"Thought you'd be a bit more excited at the big break in the case," he said. "Especially considering the upcoming election. Don't you want to capitalize on the opportunity for some good press?"

J.D. reached in his pocket for the non-existent cigarette and then folded both hands on the scarred wooden desk. "Way I see it, bringing up the Hillside Strangler case will just remind folks that it took nearly twenty-five years for us to solve." He narrowed his eyes. "I understand you'd like to see a little publicity for what tumbled in your lap, but think how much it would hurt your girlfriend if you expose her father as a murderer."

"I'm well aware of how this affects Lilah."

J.D. winked. "Then we'll keep this under our hats for now. Besides, I'll feel better about retirement knowing you're the next sheriff. I only hope your association with Lilah doesn't kill your chances. But as much as I disapprove of the Tedder gal, this is the least I can do for you."

Harlan shifted in his seat. It didn't feel right. Owing favors made his skin creepy-crawly. "Don't sit on the press for my sake."

"Why not stay quiet for now? People have assumed the killer either moved away or died. Not like there's a public outcry to find him. Besides, no matter whose prints are on the bracelet, we won't end up with a neat, tidy case. Chauncey's dead, and all we'll really have is an unproven theory."

"But Lilah could still be in danger. If Chauncey wasn't the killer, they're after her."

J.D. waved a hand, casually dismissing his concern. "They were probably after the money in that cabin incident. As for the apartment—could have been anyone or that old lady's imagination. Don't let your misplaced concern for Lilah make you any more foolish. She's caused enough trouble. For now, just sit tight and keep quiet."

For Lilah's sake, he'd go along with it. Not that his opinion mattered. J.D. did what J.D. wanted to do. Although he'd felt the same way last night about Chauncey's guilt, now he wasn't so sure. He would investigate on his own. Have a talk with that Luke McCoy and Ed.

His cell phone rang and a message flashed on its screen. Peaceful Paths Nursing Home. His stomach flipped. Now what? Had his mother taken a turn for the worse? He glanced at his desk calendar and winced.

Today would have been her thirty-fifth wedding anniversary—if Dad had bothered to hang around, that is. But he'd left the marriage, and his only child, long ago. Still, even though his mom's mind had been in a fog since her stroke and the onset of early dementia, she seemed to possess an eerie sense of this anniversary date. Last year, she'd gone into a crying funk for days, and the year before that, she'd had a series of panic attacks.

He answered the call. "Harlan Sampson speaking."

J.D.'s brows lifted as he talked to the nurse for a minute and hung up.

"Anything wrong?" he asked.

"It's Mom. Nurse says she's been weepy and asking for me."

"Poor woman. Go see her. We can hold down the fort."

"You sure?"

"Absolutely. You've accrued plenty of overtime. Take it."

Harlan stood and dug the car keys from his pants pocket. While he was in that area, might as well pay a visit to Luke McCoy and check him out. Maybe even talk to that old lady again and see if she'd seen any other unusual activity at Lilah's apartment complex.

LILAH LEFT THE sheriff's office disappointed and alone. She'd wanted to apologize to Harlan for getting so upset with him last night. Only natural that he'd pointed out the possibility of her dad's guilt. After a good night's sleep, and all morning for reflection, she'd gotten past the initial shock and her knee-jerk response to defend her dad.

She still found it hard to believe but conceded she had to consider it. And, in a way, if it were true, then she was safe. The money and jewelry were gone and she had nothing of value to anybody. Last night had been agony but today she felt ten pounds lighter. If she and the baby were truly safe, that was what mattered most. She'd never take that for granted again.

Inside her car, she punched in Aunt Vi's number on a sudden whim. She didn't want to eat lunch alone, and it would be good for Viola to get out of the house and have someone wait on *her* for a change.

It took some convincing. Vi claimed she was too busy, but Lilah at least persuaded her aunt to let her pick up some deli sandwiches in town and bring them to the house where they could eat together on the front porch. "It'll be like a picnic," she promised.

Within thirty minutes, she arrived at their house and she pulled two bacon, lettuce and cheese sandwiches from a paper bag and set them on a table. Aunt Viola supplied a bag of chips and sweet tea.

"House seems quiet," Lilah commented. "Where is everybody?"

"The kids are scattered about doing their own thing. Thad's out on a liquor run. He's having to do Ed's job now that the police are watching Ed so close. Did you know they've named him a person of interest in Darla's killing?"

Lilah sat down and unwrapped the wax packing on her sandwich. "Harlan told me. I can't believe he did it, though, can you?"

"No. But how well do we really ever know a person? Even our own family members? We all have our own mysteries and a shadowed side of the soul that's secret."

She stared at her aunt. "Wow. Does that apply to you as well? Can't imagine you having any kind of a dark side."

"Still waters run deep." She flashed a rare smile. "Your uncle can be a tad overbearing at times, so no, I'm not a self-sacrificing Pollyanna every moment of the day and night."

"Thank God. You had me worried," Lilah said with a laugh.

Viola sipped her tea. "How long you planning on staying on Lavender Mountain?"

"I'm actually thinking of leaving. Soon—like tomorrow, maybe. There's nothing to keep me here. Not now."

Her aunt patted her hand. "You've been through more

than you should have to at your young age. Especially being with child."

Lilah almost choked on her sandwich. Had she heard about the scene at the sheriff's office? "How did you guess?"

"A certain glow." Viola shrugged and smiled softly. "Are you happy about it?"

"I am now. Wasn't so sure at first. I mean, the circumstances aren't ideal."

"Harlan going to do the right thing by ya?"

"What makes you so sure it's his?"

"I see the way y'all look at each other."

Lilah cocked her head to the side. "You think he cares about me?"

"I'm certain of it."

For the first time in days, a warm glow spread through her body. If it was falsely based on an older woman's delusion, so be it. She could use a little cheer in her life.

"You'll need a strong man's protection if you're going to stay 'round here. Someone like Harlan."

"Again—I might be leaving here. Even if I did decide to stay, I don't need a man to take care of me. And if the Strangler case is solved, I have nothing to fear."

Viola's eyes widened. "Solved? What are you talking about?"

Damn. She'd let that slip. But Harlan didn't say to keep it secret. "The cops have a major break in the case. They…" She drew a deep breath. "They think Dad was the killer."

"Chauncey?" She leaned back in her chair and ran a

hand over her forehead. "Nothing should surprise me anymore when it comes to this family."

"We've had our share of tragedy, that's for sure."

"Your dad, like Thad and Jasper, had his demons. No wonder, with the father they had…" She bit her lip and stared out at the piney tree line on the side of the house.

"Grandpa Ernie?" She knew little about him. He'd died in a hunting accident before she was even born. "What about him?"

Vi's eyes were bright with tears. "You can't repeat this to anyone. I mean it."

"I won't. Go on."

"Ernest Tedder was a cruel man. He abused his three boys. And look how it turned out."

Lilah closed her eyes at the jolt of pain to think of their suffering. "Really bad?"

"The worst. Mental, physical and—damn his soul—sexual."

Lilah covered her ears with her hands, as if she could block the words already spoken. "Horrible. No wonder Dad turned to drink."

"And Jasper a recluse, and Thad—well, Thad is Thad."

Her uncle could be a little controlling, but to Lilah he seemed the most normal of the three brothers.

"And there's more," Aunt Vi continued.

Lilah wasn't sure she wanted to hear it, but better to face the problem than always wonder and imagine the unknown. "Okay, tell me."

"That hunting accident that killed Ernest…well, that was no accident."

Oh, no. Not another murder. "Please don't tell me Dad killed his own father."

"No. But you see, he isn't the only killer in the family." Viola picked at the frayed edges of her paper napkin. "Might be best if you leave town. The sooner, the better."

"But why? You implied earlier that I should marry Harlan. He's not leaving Lavender Mountain. Not ever."

Viola retreated into her shell and stuffed the wrappers and napkins in the paper sack. "Feels like there's always danger brewing in these hills. Have to admire Harlan's determination to crack down on crime if he's elected."

"He will be. Unless his association with me brings down his popularity."

"You're a fine young lady. He's lucky to have you."

Her aunt's words were balm to her troubled heart. Lilah gave her a swift hug. A twitch at the curtains caught her eye. Lavon glared through the glass pane, the smoldering anger in his eyes hot enough to scorch. Had he heard their conversation?

As always, even the barest contact with Lavon left her feeling like she needed to go home and shower. All during the drive winding down the mountain, her knuckles were white from clenching the steering wheel and her teeth ground together. All she wanted to do tonight was eat, bathe and veg out in front of the television watching romantic comedies.

Only a quarter-mile from Harlan's place she rounded the curve where a side embankment allowed vehicles to pull over for a scenic view. On impulse, she pulled in and turned off the engine. If Harlan were beside her, he'd tell her to chill. Annoying as he could be sometimes, she kind of liked the concern. She climbed out of the car, walked to the guardrail and looked—really looked—at the panoramic view.

Too often, she took the beauty of the Appalachians for granted. A thousand shades of green dotted a turquoise sky. From here, the wild Chattooga River, which served as the border between Georgia and South Carolina, appeared as a thin line of waterfalls cascading down rocky ledges and mountain draws. Its mad foaming rush to the gorges almost made her dizzy. Lilah took long slow breaths, grounding herself with the earth's energy.

A day at a time. That's how she would survive this. Yesterday's and today's sorrows didn't sentence her to a lifetime of misery. For her sake, and her child's sake, she'd take these stolen moments of peace and build happiness.

Feeling better, Lilah's gaze shifted from the distant mountain ridge back to the county road. There was a flash of sun on metal, and she did a double take. Through a slight clearing, a narrow patch of dirt road was visible. Sheriff Bentley leaned against his cruiser and Uncle Thad stepped out of his truck, pulling a wad of bills from his wallet.

Uncle Thad was supposed to be a hundred miles away in Boonesville making a big 'shine delivery. Or so he'd told Aunt Viola.

Was the sheriff a customer? She was afraid to move, afraid to draw attention to her presence. The low murmur of their voices drifted on the wind, but she couldn't discern the words. They didn't sound angry or look agitated as they conversed for a few minutes. The sheriff tucked the proffered money from Thad into his uniform shirt pocket and pressed a small envelope into her uncle's hands. Thad grinned as if he'd won the lottery and returned to his truck.

No gallon jugs of liquor exchanged.

She stood motionless, hardly daring to breathe, as the men drove off in their respective vehicles, and was relieved as they headed down the mountain instead of passing by her at the scenic overview. If they'd glimpsed her, they hadn't given any indication. Slowly, Lilah returned to her car. Her hands trembled slightly as she started the engine.

She'd never liked J.D. Bentley, and the feeling appeared to be mutual. Harlan admitted the sheriff had warned him off her. But if J.D. was so contemptuous of the Tedder name, why conduct secret business with Uncle Thad? Her best guess was that she'd witnessed a payoff to keep mum on the illegal moonshine operation. But what had J.D. given Thad in return?

Whatever had just transpired, it was probably best she didn't know. *Forget you saw it.* Chastising herself for being overly cautious, Lilah waited several minutes before pulling back out onto the road and heading down the mountain.

HARLAN ARRIVED HOME LATE, as drained as if he'd run a marathon instead of sitting for hours at the nursing home by his mom's bedside. Nothing peaceful for either of them at the Peaceful Paths facility. Between his presence and a dose of medication, they'd gotten through the hard day together.

Damn his father. Oh, the doctors wouldn't pinpoint his mom's ill health as the result of enduring his dad's abuse for years coupled with her hard work to scrape by an existence for the two of them. They would only admit stress might have been a "contributing factor."

But he knew the truth.

His house was cheerily lit and Lilah was stretched out on the sofa in front of the television set. Blond hair shadowed her face like a veil, and he sucked in his breath. He could *so* get used to this. Lilah and a baby.

But if it wasn't *his* baby…what then? Could he live with that? Would the biological father insist on being a part of Lilah's life?

Harlan entered the front door as quietly as possible, but Lilah still jerked to a sitting position and regarded him with bleary eyes.

"How's your mom?" she asked.

"Better."

She quirked a brow but didn't press for details. Good. He didn't want to talk about it, anyway. His gaze drifted down the vee of her cleavage. The impression of her nipples was plain through her thin cotton T-shirt. No bra. Was it his imagination, or were her breasts a tiny bit larger and more rounded already? His fingers twitched at his side. He wanted so badly to cup them and pull Lilah against him. She was so damn gorgeous and sexy, the only bright spot in this dark day.

"Harlan."

Her voice was husky and he swiftly raised his gaze to her face. She stepped toward him and wrapped her arms around his waist.

It was more than he'd dared hope for. He drew her to him and squeezed her petite frame against him. Close enough that she had to feel his need rubbing against her core.

Lilah moaned and pressed her hips into his arousal.

Harlan cupped her heart-shaped face in his palms and stared into gray eyes that darkened with a passion that met his own. He remembered that expression well. "Lilah?" he asked, her name harsh on his lips.

In answer, she took his hand and led him down the hallway to his bedroom.

He was out of his clothes by the time they reached the bed. His body ached as he watched Lilah lift the shirt over her head and swiftly shrug out of her jeans and panties.

She was so beautiful standing in the moonlight pouring through the window. How had he ever turned her away? He must have been out of his mind. Out of habit, he pulled open the drawer of his nightstand for a condom.

"A little late for that," she said with a breathy laugh.

"Right."

He didn't want even the thinnest barrier between the most intimate parts of their bodies. Harlan went to her, ran his hands over her breasts—definitely larger—and the soft mound of her abdomen.

"I've missed you," he said simply. "There's been nobody else."

A beat of silence hung in the air and his brain roared like thunder. This must mean she'd been with another. Which meant the baby very well might be another man's.

Or was this where she expected him to say he loved her? His tongue lay thick, heavy and unmoving in his mouth. He cleared his throat.

Feathered kisses trailed along his jaw. "You don't have to say a word," she whispered.

With that, Harlan laid her on his bed and gently kissed her forehead. "You won't be sorry, Lilah. I promise to take care of you. If you'll let me."

She pulled him against her. "Sometimes, Harlan, you talk too much."

Chapter Ten

Go or stay? Tell Harlan the truth or not?

Lilah gathered her hair into a bun at the top of her head, grabbed the water bottle and checked her cell phone. She shook her head in disgust—the battery was only at 12 percent. Probably no reception up here, anyway. She tossed it on the passenger seat and locked the car. Nothing like a walk in the woods to clear her mind and make a decision.

Only twenty yards into the Mossy Creek Trail and her jumbled emotions had lightened. The scent of cypress and pine invigorated and heightened her senses. The occasional sounds of cars passing by eventually faded and a heavy silence engulfed her, like being wrapped in a giant green cocoon.

Lilah continued on and memories of Harlan's touch last night absorbed her thoughts. It had been wild and magical—better than ever. No problem between them when it came to sex. He'd walked into the house yesterday evening and she'd instantly recognized the pain behind his smile. The one he always wore after visiting his mother. She'd gone to him at once, willing to ease his misery, no matter the cost to herself. Making love to Harlan had felt natural and right and she could no longer hide from the truth.

She still loved him.

Which left her with a decision to make. Stay and try to win his love—or leave to protect her heart and pride? The problem was, besides her own happiness, she had to consider what was best for their baby.

On she walked, sweat soaking her T-shirt as she weighed her options. The path stooped downward and a hint of running water freshened the air. Another quarter mile and she'd be at one of Dad's old stills by Mossy Creek. She glanced at the sky uneasily. Couldn't tarry too long or the path would be dark when she headed back.

A barely discernible glint of copper shimmered in the dying light, peeking out between leaves of dense mountain laurel and a patch of witch-hobble. If she hadn't known the location of her dad's still, it would have gone unnoticed. Lilah went to the brush and peeled back a limb.

Sheets of copper bonded together formed a boiler large enough to hold two hundred gallons of corn mash. Behind it was the thumper barrel, which caught the distilled alcohol as it evaporated under the heat. The clear liquid would then travel through a worm and be released out the money piece spigot where Dad used to bottle it up into gallon jugs.

Curious, Lilah knocked her fist against the steel drum. You never knew when someone in the family would take a notion to reuse one of their many old stills.

It always paid for them to keep shifting from one site to another. It kept the long arm of the law guessing. But as she'd suspected, this one gave only a hollow echo. Empty.

For the first time since her dad's death, Lilah wondered if Uncle Thad would continue on with the business. Even if he did, there was the possibility he'd lose a large portion of his customer base. Dad had been the one with the special touch for cooking up the best-tasting moonshine. Uncle Thad could mix the same ingredients of rye, barley, sugar water, yeast and wheat bran, all in the same proportions as Dad, but it didn't taste the same.

"Gots to watch it close all the time," Dad would say. "Then you gotta keep the right temperature in place, use only the freshest ingredients, know when the mash has fermented just right and then you gots to aerate it and test yer brew."

Much to Uncle Thad's chagrin, if the liquor didn't meet Dad's high standards, he would refuse to bottle and sell it. But that attention to quality had garnered them a broad and loyal customer base over the years.

She bent to untie her shoes and a gunshot ripped the air directly above her body. Shotgun pellets tore into the bark of a nearby pine and splinters cascaded like rain.

Run.

The animal instinct to flee spiked adrenaline through her body like an electrical storm. She ran blindly, with no thought of direction, only mindful to keep her body low and be less of a target. The sound of her own breath was heavy. So loud, she feared it could be heard within a mile radius.

Brambles and vines cut into her legs and arms as she trampled off the main path. A small price to pay for cover. She didn't dare look back or stop to hear if anyone approached. Another shotgun blast exploded and she ran faster. The tip of her right foot caught under a tree root and Lilah tumbled forward, jaw and nose slapping the ground. She scrambled to her feet and kept running, spitting out mouthfuls of blood—expecting any moment for a pellet to rip into her backside.

Only her breath and the pounding blood in her ears sounded for a long stretch. Was the shooter still pursuing? It felt like a knife was plunged into her left side and she leaned against a wide oak, her breathing jagged and painful.

A long shrill whistle pierced the woods.

That was no bird.

Painful or not, she had to keep going. Lilah forced her leaden legs to move forward and gasped when she came upon the mouth of a familiar cave. She hesitated, debating the wisdom of seeking shelter within its stone walls.

Another raucous whistle materialized from the opposite direction of the first one. She had to do something. Trotting in a low crouch, she broke for the cave and plunged into its darkness.

Its familiar musky scent greeted her, a reminder of childhood afternoons when she, Jimmy and Darla had played here. They'd named it Hideout Hideaway and had pretended they were pirates. The only booty they'd ever found, though, had been twenty-pound bags of grain and sugar. Jimmy had explained they were for making hooch. The cave had served as an outdoor kitchen pantry of sorts.

Lilah pressed her hands on the damp walls, making her way deep into the cave's recesses, until she reached the back wall.

There was no exit.

She sank to the ground and held her side, trying to breathe shallow and avoid the slicing pain. Had they seen her? Time crawled by while she waited to be discovered. Seconds—or perhaps minutes?—later, bass rumbles vibrated from beyond the mouth of the cave. Two male voices.

The rumble increased as they drew closer. She drew her knees into her chest and stared at the narrow entrance, which offered a view of blooming laurel and a thick clump of pine trees.

Footsteps pulsated from above—they were so close. Did they know about the cave? From their position, it would only appear to be a clump of stone.

"Where'd she go?" one of the men asked.

Lilah stuffed her knuckles in her mouth, afraid of making a sound.

"No clue."

Hold on. That voice had a familiar ring. She tried to process where she'd heard it before.

"Any idea who that woman was?"

The other man hesitated. "Maybe. Might have been one of my cousins."

Cousins? Her mind whisked as fast as a kitchen beater on high speed.

"Damn, kid. You a coldhearted one shootin' at kin."

"Kin or not, they ain't got no business 'round here."

"I reckon you scared her off, no harm done." The man paused a heartbeat. "That's all you were doin' right? Scaring her?"

"Right," the familiar voice answered.

He lied. Lilah could tell it by the flat, hard inflection of his voice.

"Let's head on back, be getting dark soon."

A shotgun blast unexpectedly erupted and Lilah clamped her hands over her ears.

The men laughed.

"If you can hear me, take warning," the man shouted. "Stay away from here and mind yer own business."

Would she ever.

Mercifully, the footsteps resumed, heading away.

Whew. She leaned her head against the cool damp stone and waited for her thrumming heart to settle. Had Dad and Uncle Thad always kept someone on guard near their still? Strange how she'd never associated the moonshine operation with violence. Yes, it was illegal and yes, the state sent tobacco, alcohol and firearm agents scouring the mountains once every few years, but it had never crossed her mind that protecting the still meant shooting anyone who stumbled across it.

Her mouth tightened in anger. Uncle Thad be damned. Soon as she got back to Harlan's, she'd report the location and have this still—and the others—shut down once and for all. Those old monsters of welded copper and steel had caused enough pain in the family. No point in some wandering, innocent tourist being killed over that metal apparatus someday.

Might have been one of my cousins one of the men had stated.

She had a good many second and third cousins scattered over the county, but Lilah's mind leaped to her first cousin. Lavon.

Definitely Lavon. They'd never gotten along—but did he really hate her enough to want her dead? She recalled the cold, hard set to his eyes when she'd caught him eavesdropping on her conversation with Uncle Thad.

She rose to leave the cave, but her legs shook too bad to support her weight. Anger melted, leaving a crippling paralysis in its wake. Lilah sank back down onto the damp ground. A little more time to rest and get herself together, then she would head home. Must have run faster and farther than she'd thought. No matter how many deep breaths she tried to take, her lungs demanded more oxygen. And her heart issued its own brutal demand, a rapid and incessant pumping.

Calm down. This would pass. A few more minutes…

…Only it didn't pass. Surely, she was too young for a heart attack. The baby. Had she damaged her unborn child? *Don't go there.* Yet, the worry festered and the more she tried to dismiss it, the more it loomed. Lilah placed one hand on her heart and the other on her stomach, willing mind and body to slow down. *We're safe*, she repeated like a mantra.

A bit of the tension eased. It was working. Lilah gingerly sank down and rested her entire body on the slab of stone. Closing her eyes, she melded into the darkness and the protection of the cave's thick unyielding walls. Just a little rest before she left its shelter. A little more time to quiet her heart, revive her legs and let Lavon and the other guy move out of the area.

WHERE WAS SHE?

Harlan paced the den and tried to ring her cell phone for the hundredth time, but there was no answer. He walked through the house again, checking tables and counters for a note. Lilah knew he would worry if she was unaccounted for.

Something was wrong. Outside, the shadows had darkened and deepened to the point they were almost indistinguishable in the evening's landscape.

He wasn't taking any chances. What good was it working in law enforcement if you couldn't pull a few strings? Quickly, he dialed the county dispatcher and set up an APB for Lilah's car. Next, he called the landlord of her apartment building in case she'd returned there.

His stomach took a dive. Had she left him for good? Yes, they'd made love last night, and it had been amazing, but he hadn't said the words she'd needed to hear. Maybe she'd finally had enough—had grown weary waiting on him to get his act together.

He couldn't sit in this empty house and imagine worst-case scenarios involving Lilah. Harlan hightailed it to the cruiser and kept the police scanner on as he sped to Thaddeus Tedder's place. With any luck, Lilah was visiting kin and the time had slipped away from her. He flipped on the blue siren switch and climbed the mountain.

The moment he pulled into the driveway, disappointment washed over him. Lilah's car was nowhere in sight.

He parked on a diagonal just by the porch where Thaddeus, his wife and their eldest son sat. The cherry from Thad's cigar glowed and moths fluttered around the overhead light.

"You seen Lilah?" he asked without preamble, exiting the car.

Thad spoke for the group. "Not today. Why?"

Viola started to rise from her rocking chair. "She in some kind of trouble?"

"Only trouble she's in is from our deputy here," their son joked.

Everyone kept assuming he was the father. If only he could be as certain. Harlan's hands went to his hips and he glared at the guy—Lavon, if he was remembering correctly. Punk kid. The name Lavon Tedder had come up a few times over the years. All minor incidents—a school fight, petty theft, vandalism. Never could pin anything on him, though; kid was as slippery as his dad. How had Lilah risen above this despicable family?

"Lavon!"

Even in the darkness, Viola's red face was evident.

"When you going to do right by Lilah?" Thad smirked, ignoring his son's rude comment. "Although, if you ask me, she can do lots better than a do-good nobody like you. Told her so, too."

Nobody had asked Thad's opinion. Coming here had been a complete waste of time.

"You hear from Lilah, let me know."

"Can't keep tabs on your own woman?" Lavon mocked.

That did it. "What's your problem, kid? Two people in your family are dead and Lilah's unaccounted for."

"He didn't mean nothing by it," Thad said. "She's probably just visiting a friend."

Harlan wished he could believe in a simple explanation. He also wished for a crime free community, prosperity in Appalachia and world peace. But wishing didn't make it so.

"Let's hope that's the case." He returned to the cruiser and got in, ready to pull out, when Viola came to the door and motioned for him to roll down the window.

"Call me when you find her." Her face taut. "Lilah's always been one to hike out in the woods, alone, but she don't need to be running around at night all by herself."

"Under the circumstances, I couldn't agree with you more."

Harlan drove back to the main road. What next? Lilah claimed to have lost touch with old childhood friends, which just left family. She hadn't gone to visit Ed or her nephews—he'd already checked. And she wasn't with her elderly aunt—he'd called there, too. Which only left Jasper Tedder. The old coot would be even less happy to see him than Thad, not that it mattered.

Darkness seeped in by degrees as he climbed to the top of Lavender Mountain, and with it a heavy blanket of dread weighed on his heart. He had to find Lilah soon. What if she were out in the woods and had turned her ankle—or something worse? Over ten years as a deputy sheriff had provided too many horrific examples of tragic accidents and crimes.

His cruiser headlights pierced the ramshackle building Jasper called home. It was slapped together from sheets of pressed wood and sported a rusty tin roof—

one stiff wind away from annihilation. The porch was haphazardly strewn with an ironing board, an old school desk, boxes and plastic bins. Harlan parked and got out of the vehicle.

Jasper stalked out the front door waving his arms. "My peppers!"

Huh? Harlan scanned the premises.

"You run over my pepper plants."

Harlan looked back and, sure enough, he'd driven over a couple. "Sorry, sir. I'll come back out later this week with new plants."

Jasper rubbed at his beard. "I reckon that'll be all right then. See that you do."

"Yes, sir. I came to ask if you'd heard from Lilah today."

White scraggly eyebrows lifted. "She don't come to call very often. Why you asking?"

"It's late and getting dark. She usually lets me know if she won't be home for dinner."

"Well, now don't you paint a nice cozy picture. Fact is, son, you're living in sin with my niece. You can pretty it up any way you please but facts is facts. The Lord don't—"

"If you don't mind, sir. Have you seen Lilah or not?"

"Not today. Maybe she's come to her senses and gone back to her own place like a nice respectable young lady. Back in my day, we didn't cotton to this foolishness of make-believe marriages and such. Far as I'm concerned, y'all are playing house."

He'd been lectured enough today. "The point is— Lilah might be in danger."

The walkie-talkie belted by his hip crackled and the dispatcher's voice sounded: *Navy blue compact car located. License plate ALA34892. Registered owner listed as Lilah Tedder. Found by entrance to Mossy Creek Trail. Vehicle is unoccupied.*

Damn. Adrenaline flushed his body. What was she doing there? Something bad had happened to her, he just knew it, had felt it all along. Harlan rushed to his car.

"She really in danger?" Jasper sprinted to the passenger's side and climbed in. "I'm going with you. I know that area like the back of my hand."

Harlan hit the gas and turned on the blue light. Mossy Creek had once been a popular path leading to the main Appalachian Trial but he hadn't walked it since he was a teenager.

"Why are you so familiar with this trail?" he asked Jasper. He doubted Lilah's uncle would be much help, but engaging in conversation would help keep the turmoil at bay.

"I have my reasons. Enough said."

Harlan gritted his teeth. Jasper could be maddening. Stubborn as all get-out. If he didn't want to volunteer information, nothing could pry it loose. But right now, he didn't much care how Jasper came to know that neck of the woods as long as he proved helpful.

He pressed the redial number for Lilah's phone on the off-chance she'd called, but he got the same empty ring and the same voice-mail message. In disgust, he dropped it in the console.

Jasper picked it up, palming the phone as if it were

an alien object dropped from outer space. "How you work this thing?"

"Now's not a good time for me to bring you into the twenty-first century," he said, rounding a curve a little too fast and fishtailing back into his own lane.

"I'm gonna git us some help. Walk me through the process."

Every law enforcement officer in the county would be there, but if Lilah was lost or hurt in the woods, every person on patrol mattered.

"Press the button on the side and then touch the phone receiver icon."

"Icon?"

"Little picture on the screen."

Harlan slowed down. He couldn't afford an accident along the way.

"Now what?" Jasper asked.

"Press the dial pad option." At Jasper's perplexed expression, Harlan sighed and pulled off to the side of the road. "Just give it to me. What's the number?"

"Don't have to git huffy."

Jasper rattled off the number and Harlan punched it out before returning the phone to him. A ring echoed over the Bluetooth radio connection as he pulled back onto the road.

"Hello," a gruff voice answered.

"Thad? Git out to Mossy Creek Trail and bring anyone you can find for a search-and-rescue."

Jasper spoke loudly, the phone held close to his ear, and Harlan didn't bother explaining that was unnecessary.

"Lilah's car's stranded out there. Our gal's missing."

They arrived at the scene within ten minutes. Three police cars and a state trooper vehicle were already there. Bile rose in his throat at the sight of officers shining their flashlights inside Lilah's abandoned car. Was she in the car and possibly hurt?

Harlan slammed on his brakes, inches from a parked cop car, and hurried over. "What's happening?"

J.D. placed a hand on his shoulder. "No sign of any blood or a struggle. With any luck, she just went for a walk and got lost. We'll find her."

"She left her phone in the car." Officer Alvin Lee honed his flashlight on the passenger's seat where Lilah's phone lay.

"We've got to find her—organize a search," Harlan said.

"We're on it." The nearby state trooper stepped over and held out a hand. "Harlan Sampson? Trooper Davis. Understand the subject is your girlfriend?"

"Correct." Harlan absently shook his hand.

"Called for a helicopter search-and-rescue mission. In light of the recent murders, approval shouldn't be a problem."

"Thank you." Finally, a piece of good news.

More cars arrived and the night filled with the sounds of people shouting commands and the crackle of static and disembodied voices from police scanners. Blue lights strobed over the scene while officers donned headlamp gear and dug out first-aid kits. Most were no strangers to these missions. Tourists got lost, or hikers

on the Appalachian Trail sustained injuries and failed
to report to their next checkpoint, alarming their next of
kin. He'd always felt compassion for the waiting, worried families, never imagining he'd live through this
particular agony himself.

Sammy clamped a hand on his shoulder. "Hang in
there, buddy. Lilah's a mountain girl, born and raised.
She'll be fine."

"I'm going with you."

Sammy thrust a headlamp, a whistle on a chain and
a compass at him. "Figured as much." He looked past
Harlan's shoulders and whistled. "Take a look at this."

People streamed from dozens of parked cars. Jasper
rounded them together with the help of a cop as they
organized a search.

For the first time in the past two frustrating hours,
Harlan's throat closed up and he blinked hard. That's
what he loved about Lavender Mountain. That's what
made this place home. Everyone came together in times
of need—without question and without complaint. He
recalled nights when he and his mom—for days in a
row—were down to nothing but grits for dinner. Some
kind anonymous neighbors would leave them a basket
of fresh-baked food or a casserole dish warm from their
oven.

Harlan strapped on the headlamp, placed the whistle
chain around his neck and joined his fellow officers at
the head of the trail. Six-by-six, they entered and walked
in a horizontal line, their combined lights illuminating
the forest like a blazing wall.

They would find her, alive and well. He refused to accept any other possibility.

I'm coming for you, Lilah. Hang on.

Chapter Eleven

A storm of turbulence thundered through the mountain. Lilah was startled awake, bewildered and fearful. Damp stone, darkness and the metallic tinge of blood in her mouth reminded her of the afternoon's events. But what was that roaring cacophony? From the cave's mouth, a monochromic flash of white beams lit the trees. Faraway voices wafted faintly.

She slowly rose and walked on wobbling legs to the entrance, then leaned against the stone aperture. Ahead, a helicopter drew nearer before circling and hovering almost directly above. She blinked, adjusting from the cave's darkness and silence to the piercing light and noise.

They were looking for *her*. She'd been part of search-and-rescue missions before, although never at night. And she'd certainly never been the objective of one.

"Here," she called. But her voice was weak, certainly not audible over the chopper's engine.

A ray of light from above shone directly on her body and she blinked and waved her arms.

"Lilah!"

She distinctly heard her name and turned her head to the right.

Harlan ran toward her, his eyes frantic. "Are you hurt? You're bleeding."

Without waiting for an answer, he picked her up and cradled her against his broad chest, which she buried her face in, shutting out the commotion. She inhaled the scent of clean linen blended with a woodsy note, savoring the comfort and strength of Harlan's presence.

Now she had the answer she'd been seeking when she'd entered the forest hours ago. No way was she leaving this man or this mountain. He deserved to know the truth. He was the father of her child and she loved and trusted him. She'd never stopped loving him, even when he'd withdrawn his affection after her spring break was over.

"We'll get you to a hospital right away," he vowed, stroking her hair. "What happened? Did somebody hurt you or did you just take a tumble?"

Before she could answer, Jasper ran up to them. "Lay-Lay, you okay little girl?"

"I'm fine now."

The harsh lines of her uncle's face relaxed. "Had a hunch you'd head out to this cave when they found your car at the trail entrance. You always did love to play in it when you were a kid. You and Jimmy and Darla, too."

Ah, so that's how they knew where to search. "Thank you, Uncle Jasper."

They were quickly surrounded by others. Spontaneous cheers erupted from the volunteers. Lilah recognized Sammy and Alvin as they pushed their way over.

"What happened, Lilah?" Sammy asked.

She shot Harlan an uneasy glance. "I came out for a walk and two men took shots at me. Sounded like a shotgun. I ran to the cave and hid."

Harlan's arms and chest tightened, hardening against her body.

Alvin gave a low whistle. "Why would they shoot at you?"

Her eyes slid involuntarily to Jasper and he gave the slightest shake of his head, as if asking her to keep quiet. He always called moonshine the "devil's brew," but family was family and they stuck together.

"Who were the bastards?" Harlan's face was pinched and his question clipped. "That's what I need to know."

"I—I can't say for sure. I never saw them, just heard their voices later, outside the cave." Hell, she hated to tell him this next part. "I waited a long time before trying to leave, but my heart was racing and I was exhausted from running. I lay down to rest and then—" she waved an arm at the chaos. "—then I woke to the sound of the chopper."

"You didn't recognize the voices?"

Of course, Harlan cut right to the heart of the matter. She hesitated, unwilling to implicate Lavon in front of everyone. Could she really be one hundred percent positive it was him without having seen his face? If it wasn't Lavon, she'd do him a great disservice by casting blame. And her family would be furious.

"Maybe," she conceded, lowering her voice so only Harlan could hear. "I'll tell you later. All right?"

He looked as if he wanted to argue, but relented when

she cupped his jaw in her palms. "Please, I'm tired. I just want to go home. Okay? We can talk there—alone."

Sammy interrupted. "Any injuries other than your split lip? Do you need to go to the hospital?"

"No. No hospital."

Harlan frowned. "Can you walk?"

Lilah spied the sheriff striding toward them with his usual air of impatience, his features stern and implacable. He didn't appear glad to see her one whit. Probably angry she'd created such a stir and cost the good taxpayers' money and time.

"Yes, I can walk." She wiggled out of his arms and stood. "Let's get outta here."

J.D. pulled out his walkie-talkie and informed the helicopter pilot that the mission was accomplished and the person found didn't need a hospital emergency escort. He eyed her with his usual faint air of condescension. "Why were you out walking so late in this area?" he asked in a you-should-know-better tone.

"Didn't know that was a crime." He prickled her temper. But the truth was, she felt guilty. She didn't want to think about how much it cost for a chopper search.

"No crime. Seems strange, though. Girl like you should know the dangers of roaming the forest at night."

"It wasn't dark when I started," she snapped. "And how was I supposed to know I'd get shot at?"

"You saying someone shot at you?" His tone held just a tinge of disbelief.

"Why would I lie?"

Harlan jumped in the fray, squeezing her hand before

addressing his boss. "It's late and we're all tired. You'll have a full statement from Lilah in the morning, J.D."

"See that I do."

HARLAN GENTLY DABBED a washcloth at the gash on Lilah's mouth, relieved to find the cut was superficial and didn't even need stitches. Had to hurt like hell, though. Who had done this to her? He tamped down the anger. That could wait. For now, he wanted to take care of Lilah and ease her mind. She stood before him in the shower, the bubbles from her bath gel enticingly covering her rosy skin.

Harlan groaned inwardly at the temptation. Tonight was hardly the time to make love. "Go ahead and get under the spigot so I can wash your hair."

"I'm okay. Could have done this myself," she grumbled but, nevertheless, stepped into the tub of steaming water.

"Thanks for humoring me."

He squirted a dollop of shampoo in his palm and began kneading it into her hair. The feel of the lather in her long blond hair and the flowery smell created a tender sense of intimacy.

"Have to admit this feels like heaven," she said breathily, eyes closed.

Good. This also gave him a chance to more thoroughly check out her naked body for other signs of injury. So far, only scraped knees. His stomach lurched at the thought of how horrible it could have been. If he'd lost Lilah... No, best not to go there.

He rinsed her hair and wrapped a towel around her

head. She stepped out of the tub and he gently dried her off. As always, the sight of her naked body was arousing, but tonight it was also tempered with a deep tenderness.

"I'm sorry to be so much trouble." She blinked back tears. "I got everybody riled up tonight, especially J.D."

He followed her into the bedroom where she pulled on a pink nightgown and plopped on the bed.

"Screw J.D. Everyone else was concerned about your safety, not angry."

"He's not wrong. It was stupid to go out there so late in the afternoon. Although, in my defense, I got so spent after running that I couldn't hike back to the car. Plus, it's weird. Inside the cave, even once I knew they were gone, my heart started racing. No matter how much I rested, it felt like I couldn't breathe."

"Might have been a panic attack."

"That makes me sound like a weakling—a hysterical female." Lilah removed the towel from her head and starting working a comb through her long locks.

"No way. You were attacked in the woods and were alone and pregnant. Would have been a wonder if you hadn't panicked. Nobody is judging you for anything. As for being in the woods, you couldn't have known two psychos were roaming about. Speaking of which—it's time to tell me everything."

She sighed. "Right. Remember, it's all just supposition, though, as far as the shooters. That's why I didn't mention it in front of everybody. Darla, Jimmy and I used to play in that cave as kids because it was near one of Dad's old stills. While he worked, we entertained ourselves there. The second I heard the shotgun blast, I instinctively ran to it. While I was hiding, I heard two men talking on the ground above me."

His jaw tightened. "What did they say? Any idea who they were?"

"One asked the other if he'd only shot to scare me away and the other man said he had, but I think he lied. And the worst part is…the man that lied? It might have been my cousin Lavon."

He'd get the truth out of Lavon in the morning—no matter what it took. "I wouldn't put it past that guy. But why would he shoot at you?"

"Maybe he did it to protect the still location? Or maybe just out of plain meanness?"

"You said it was an old still, so that seems unlikely. Unless they're using it again?"

She winced at a tangle in her hair and set the comb on the nightstand. "No. I checked underneath and there haven't any recent fires lit for cooking moonshine."

Harlan rose and went to the window, gazing at the dark sky. To think she'd been alone and vulnerable out there made his gut clench. Damn if he wouldn't get to the bottom of this first thing in the morning. He'd have Lavon spilling his guts before noon.

"The Tedders *are* trouble. Except for you," he quickly amended. "They wanted to hurt—or scare you—for a reason. I aim to find out why."

"But I could be wrong about Lavon," she added hastily. "I didn't see him so I can't swear in a court of law he was the one. What if I'm wrong? Much as I dislike him, I don't want him locked up on a false charge. And Uncle Thad and Aunt Vi would never forgive me, either."

"You've been through enough without worrying about their feelings."

She bit her lip. "Lavon will be really angry. Whether he's innocent or not."

"I won't let him get to you."

"You can't protect me twenty-four seven."

"Can we at least agree that, until everything settles down, you don't go anywhere alone?"

"I won't go walking alone in the woods again. Probably ever."

She hadn't exactly agreed to his terms, but he couldn't keep her under lock and key, either. "At least promise me that if you leave the house while I'm at work, you'll let me know where you're going?"

"Agreed." She flashed the first real smile he'd seen from her today. "See? I can be reasonable."

Whew. He sat beside her on the bed and ran a hand through his hair. He couldn't be worrying about her safety when he needed a clear head to ponder the possibilities of what was behind the shooting. He'd question Lavon, then go back out to the old still and the cave to look around. Those men were guarding something. If not moonshine, was it drugs? His heart beat faster, the way it did when he was onto something. That area was perfect—off the beaten path but close enough to a main road for easy access to transportation.

"Did you see anything suspicious in that cave?"

"I didn't look. There's several narrow passages in the back, but I've always avoided them. Bats, you know. Why? You think there's something hidden?"

"Could be."

Lilah grinned. "We always knew there was hidden treasure in there."

"I call it contraband, if it's what I suspect it is. I'll know in the morning."

"Drugs? Could be. I want to go with you tomorrow."

"No way. This will be official police work. We can't let civilians come along."

"Please? I think it would help me to go back there in daylight. I'll go crazy just sitting around your home all day."

"J.D. would raise hell."

"So don't tell him. That man's a crook. How can you stand to work for him?"

"I realize you don't like him and I can't blame you. But come on—a crook?"

"I can't prove it, but yeah, I have my suspicions."

He regarded her evenly. J.D. could be an ass. Could her dislike for him be coloring her opinion of his integrity? "Go on. Why?"

"Just the other day I saw Uncle Thad give a him a large roll of money. They were pulled over to the side of the road in an area overgrown with trees and brush—an area sheltered from public view."

Harlan frowned. "Maybe J.D. bought something from him?"

"The only thing I saw exchange hands was my uncle handing him money and then J.D. slipped him an envelope."

That didn't sound good. A local sheriff receiving money from a known moonshiner? Still, he had to be fair. "I'll ask J.D. about it. He might have bought a large-ticket item from Thad and then your uncle gave him a receipt. Something explainable."

"More likely J.D.'s on the take to turn a blind eye."

If his boss was accepting money to keep quiet about moonshining, what was to keep him from doing the same with illegal drug operations? Could he be the one tipping off the distributors before a raid? If he was, they had a real mess on their hands.

Lilah's mouth twisted. "Can you leave my name out of it when you ask J.D. about the money? He's already unhappy with me. Makes me uneasy to tick off the sheriff."

"Don't worry," he admonished, wanting her to relax and have a good night's rest after her ordeal. Everything else could wait until morning. "All's well. You have the sheriff's deputy wrapped around your little finger."

"Do I?" she asked wistfully, cocking her head to the side.

"How can you not know that?" he asked roughly. He'd opened his home to her, despite the fact it was probably the worst thing in the world for him career-wise.

Her lips tugged at the corners and she held up both hands, ticking off the reasons why on her fingers. "One: because you've never told me you loved me. Two: because I'm bad news for your dream job. And three: because I'm pregnant."

All true. And yet, he couldn't deny that she sent his emotions on a tailspin like no other woman had ever done.

"I love you, Harlan," she said simply. Her eyes shone like pewter.

"I—I care about you." He closed his eyes and tried to

order his jumbled thoughts. Could he make this work?
Marry a Tedder—one possibly pregnant by another man
of all things—and still win the election?

But even if he became the next sheriff, without Lilah
by his side, it would be a hollow victory. He was confused, yes, but he knew one thing: he wanted her here
with him. To protect her from any harm. Forever.

Only one way to do that. He slid down the mattress
and planted one knee on the floor.

"Marry me, Lilah."

She sucked in air and a hand flew to her chest.
"But…" She glanced down at her belly.

"I don't care who the father is. I mean, yes, I care,
but even if the baby's not mine, I want you, Lilah. What
do you say?"

In less than a heartbeat, she was in his arms, her fingers raking his hair, pulling him toward her in a kiss.
Her mouth was urgent and pliant against his. The press
of her body and the smell of her skin mixed with the
soap and the shampoo were like a drug. He could never
get enough of Lilah. Not ever. Their bodies sank onto
the bed and he leaned on his elbows, taking in the sight
of her flushed with passion.

"I take it that's a *yes*?"

A THOUSAND TIMES YES.

In answer, she kissed him again and wiggled her hips
against his erection. He might not be able to say the
words yet, but he loved her. Whatever messed up hell
his dad had put him through growing up, Harlan had
a great capacity for love. He'd just proved it by asking

her to marry him when he believed her pregnant by another. One day, he would recognize his feelings for what they truly were.

His mouth captured one of her nipples and he suckled while one hand traveled up her inner thigh, hot and demanding. She gasped as one of his fingers entered her core and began moving in and out. He knew just where to touch, where to press and how hard. Lilah broke away and quickly helped him tug out of his jeans. He was as ready as she was and he thrust inside her, the tension building between them in a familiar intimate storm. She came first, and then she floated back down, watching the tense lines of his face and the darkening of his eyes as he reached his own climax.

He rolled off her and she snuggled against his side. Together, their labored breathing relaxed to normal. Lilah traced the strong plane of his jaw and cheekbones.

Now was the time.

"Harlan?" she began tentatively, suddenly nervous.

In response, he took her hand and kissed her fingers, his gaze intense.

"I have something to tell you."

"Go on."

"The baby's yours," she whispered.

He didn't move, other than the widening of his eyes.

She'd expected more. A smile, a hug…something. "Is that okay?" she asked nervously.

Harlan eased back and propped up on his elbows, studying her.

She bit her lip. "There hasn't been anyone else for me,

either. I didn't want to tell you earlier because, well, I didn't want you to feel like you had to marry me."

"You lied to me." His voice was hard and unbending. "All this time. You left me wondering. Do you have any idea what it's been like?"

Oh, hell. She'd ruined everything. "I'm sorry. Can we—maybe start over again?"

Harlan was out of the bed in a heartbeat, picking up his tossed clothes in angry swiping movements. She'd never seen him like this before, as if he couldn't even bear to look at her.

"Just wipe the slate clean, huh?" he snapped. "Forget you lied to me?"

She sat up, gathering the bedsheet over her breasts. "I'm willing if you are."

He glared at her. "I bet."

Her own temper rose. "You haven't exactly been blameless yourself. You broke off with me because you didn't think I was good enough for you."

"Not true."

His face flushed, whether from anger or guilt she couldn't say.

"It *is* true," she insisted. "You as much as admitted it the other day."

"My qualm wasn't with you, it was with your family."

"Same thing."

He walked out.

Lilah hugged her knees to her chest, feeling as disoriented as when she'd been lost in the woods. To go from the happiest moment of her life to the silent aftermath of a fight left her shaken.

It's going to be okay, she promised herself. He just needs to cool off a bit and come to grips with the news. After all, she'd had weeks to come to terms with the situation. By morning, this may well have blown over.

Chapter Twelve

It hadn't blown over.

Breakfast had been civil, but decidedly cool. He'd left for work and returned home a couple of hours later, offering to take her to the cave with him. A peace offering, she'd hoped. But on the drive out, Harlan looked about as solemn as she'd ever seen. Maybe coming along to the cave wasn't such a hot idea. "You want another cup of coffee?" she asked, holding up the thermos like an olive branch.

"No more caffeine. I just want to throttle your cousin Lavon. That's all."

At least he was directing his ire elsewhere. "I always feel that way about him. I take it you talked to him this morning?"

"Tried to. He denied shooting at you. Claimed he was nowhere near the cave yesterday."

Doubts assailed her mind. Had she been wrong? She'd been distraught last night. Maybe her dislike of Lavon had tainted her judgment. "Let it go, then. I can't prove it and there's a chance I'm wrong."

"I'm not letting it go. No way. Told Lavon I was keep-

ing an eye on him and if he ever came at you again that…
Well, never mind the details. At least I managed to shake
up his smug expression a little near the end. Said he was
telling his dad that I'd harassed him." Harlan snorted.
"As if I'm scared of Thaddeus Tedder."

She wished she'd kept her mouth shut about her suspicions. Now things would be all awkward with Aunt
Vi and Uncle Thad. Lilah sighed and looked out the car
window for the rest of the drive.

"Sure you want to go back out there?" Harlan pulled
off the road at the Mossy Creek Trail entrance.

"Positive."

Anything was better than sitting around fretting.
She'd give her aunt and uncle a few days to simmer
down about this mess and then pay them a visit. She
unbuckled her seat belt and stepped out of the cruiser.

A few strewn cigarette butts and some tossed plastic cups near the trail opening were a reminder of last
night's ordeal. Lilah took a deep breath and headed into
the woods. She was damn lucky to be alive and walking this same path.

Harlan stepped beside her, his expression still som-
ber. He seemed so…remote and official, wearing his
stiff brown uniform. Unapproachable, even.

She forced some cheer into her voice. "This might be
fun. Who knows what we'll find in that cave? Jimmy,
Darla and me were convinced it held treasure."

"When you were still old enough to believe in the
Tooth Fairy and Santa Claus?" A trace of a smile hovered on his lips.

"Not just any old treasure. Pirate's treasure—gold, swords, doubloons."

"Those were some crazy lost pirates if they wandered from shore all the way to the North Georgia Mountains."

Nothing seemed impossible when they had been little. Her throat closed shut remembering Darla's face when she'd found a necklace Jimmy had planted for her in the cave. She'd squealed in excitement, dancing a jig and laughing. She always had liked pretty baubles. A shame she hadn't owned more of them in her short life.

Lilah fanned her face. It was warming up quick. How could Harlan stand walking around in that hot uniform?

"Oh, there's the old still down in the draw if you want to take a look at it," she said, pointing at the location.

"Might as well."

They walked down to the creek and she led him to it, fighting back a bit of guilt. If her father could see her now… But he was dead. Maybe exposing all their dirty family secrets would lead to finding his and Darla's killer.

Harlan bent down and picked up the plastic water bottle. "This yours?"

"Yeah. I stopped to tie my shoelaces when I heard the first shot. Forgot all about the water and hightailed it that way." She pointed eastward.

"Doesn't the main trail take you to the cave?"

"I was in a bit of a hurry," she said drily.

"Of course. I want to retrace your steps, though. You don't need to go through these brambles. I can meet you at the cave."

"No way," she said with a snort. "I'm not walking there alone."

"Fine, you can help me. Keep your eyes peeled for shotgun shells. Which way did you run after you dropped the bottle?"

She pointed straight ahead and he walked forward, with Lilah in tow. Nearly a hundred feet later, he retrieved a plastic casing from the ground. "Here's one of them."

"Will it do you any good?"

"Some. We can check the firing ping marks on the shotgun shell's primer for microscopic identification— see if it matches a particular shotgun."

"That's the best news I've heard all day." Now they were getting somewhere.

"Don't get too excited. All it can really do, legally, is exclude certain guns."

Her shoulders sagged. "Then what good is it?"

"We can get a search warrant for Lavon's guns and run a ballistics test. If the firing pin markings match up, then I'd say we have our first circumstantial evidence pointing to your cousin. Not that we can arrest him without other proof."

"At least we're headed in the right direction."

Through a thick layer of pine needles, her right foot stepped on something hard. Lilah bent and brushed away the needles, picking up another shell. The plastic casing sent tremors up her arm and made her heart skitter. How close had she come to serious injury or death—a couple feet? A few inches? She placed her hands over her stomach.

"You okay?"

Harlan came up behind her and wrapped his arms

around her waist, his palms covering her fingers. There, together, their hands lay entwined against her belly where their unborn child grew. Peace washed over her and with it, last night's sorrow. Lilah squeezed her eyes shut and soaked in the sacred intimacy of the moment. She and their baby were safe. Harlan might not recognize his own feelings yet, but this was love. As pure as it got. Eventually, he would realize it on his own.

"I'm fine, Harlan." She turned and pressed her face into his chest a moment before stepping away. "Let's get this guy. Both of them. Maybe today will be the first real break in the case."

He held up crossed fingers. "Your optimism's rubbing off. Could be we get lucky and find something else in the cave."

She high-fived him and they picked their way through the shrubs for several minutes. The stone walls of the cave appeared suddenly.

"There it is. Hideout Hideaway."

"Good thing Jasper led us here last night. Even on the main trail, it's not easy to see behind those huge spruce and river birches." Harlan handed her a flashlight. "Ready?"

In answer, she turned on the flashlight and walked inside. The drop in temperature felt refreshing, although yesterday evening it had gotten a bit chilly. Thank heavens she hadn't been forced to spend the night here.

"What's this?"

Harlan strode to the west side where faint red markings splattered the wall.

"I can't believe it's still there!" Lilah laughed and

shone her flashlight on it. "Take three kids and a can of red paint. We had a blast until Dad collected us to go home." She ran a finger over the faint marks. "There's my initials."

Harlan squinted. "Yeah, I see it now. Cool. But show me those side passages you mentioned."

"You're going to get your uniform all messed up," she warned.

"Doesn't matter."

She led him back to the first passage. "This is the smallest one. You'd have to crawl through it. I never did, but Jimmy went a little ways in it once."

Harlan shone the flashlight. "Hmm. Don't see anything here. Doesn't look promising. I'll come back later with Sammy for this one and bring rope. Where's another one?"

"This one's the largest," she said, taking him farther into the cave's recesses. "It's narrow but tall. We won't even have to stoop to walk to the end of the passage."

Harlan led the way and came to an abrupt halt. "Well, looka here."

He stooped down and she peered over his bent figure. A dozen empty plastic baggies littered the ground.

"Looks like trash to me."

"If it's what I think it is…" He put on a pair of gloves and picked one up. Little crumbles of dried leaf and buds were tucked in the corners.

"Is that—" she began.

"Yup. Marijuana."

He shone the flashlight farther into the rock tunnel. "I see a bigger bundle."

He went over and picked up a book-sized package wrapped in cardboard and bundled in twine.

"Open it," she breathed, skin tingling with anticipation.

"Nope. Going to take this back to work, open it there and get it logged into the chain of evidence."

"So that's why those men shot at me. I got too close to their drugs."

"Must be a big-time operation for them to go to those lengths. I suspect this cave's a temporary holding place until transport. Ideally, you'd store marijuana in a dry room."

He directed the flashlight beam at the wet ground where the mud was imprinted with large footprints. "Bet at the crack of dawn they were in here and removed all they could."

Lilah shuddered, suddenly eager to get away. She'd had enough excitement for one day—for a lifetime, actually.

J.D.'s FACE WAS nearly purple with anger.

"What the hell have you been up to this morning, Harlan? First, I get a call from Thaddeus Tedder threatening legal action against our office for harassing his son, and now you tell me you've been trampling through the woods with a civilian?"

This wasn't what he'd been expecting. Not at all. He didn't think J.D. would be *happy* that he'd struck out on his own this morning, but he *had* found drug evidence they'd been searching for these past couple of years. It wasn't much, but it was a start.

"I was careful. Everything was done by the book. Now that we know what's out there—"

"By the book? Are you kidding me?" J.D. shoved the cardboard bundle away from him. "This is worthless to us now."

"I followed protocol," Harlan said stiffly. "I used gloves, took a couple photos with my cell phone and then bagged the evidence. I'll have it all in my report."

J.D. clutched the edge of his desk, white-knuckled. "Forget the report. I'll head out there myself with the narcotics dogs and a team. Meanwhile, I want you to take a week off work. Effective immediately."

What the hell? Harlan blinked. "I don't want a vacation. I want to work this case."

"At this point, I don't care what you want. That time off wasn't a suggestion, it's an order."

"Why are you doing this?"

"You're letting that woman run you in circles. You're so in lust that you've lost your judgment and any sense of perspective." He shook his head in disgust. "Running all over the mountain accusing people of crimes on nothing but hearsay, then striking out on your own at a crime scene and taking your girlfriend along with you. Take a week off and think about it."

"I don't need to think about." Harlan worked to keep his voice down. J.D. was still his boss after all. "Lavon Tedder is a punk. Look at his juvenile record and—"

"I know who the hell he is. Doesn't mean you can run roughshod over the guy."

"You've got to be kidding me." How many times had

he witnessed J.D. doing the same? "We have a witness who's almost certain she heard his voice after an attack."

"*Almost?* Not like your girlfriend actually saw Lavon."

Harlan picked up the baggie with the collected shotgun shells and waved them at J.D. "She was almost killed. You really going to let this slide because Lavon went crying to his daddy? We need to get a subpoena for his guns and run a ballistics test to see if they match the shell casings."

"That won't hold up in a court of law and you know it."

"Doesn't mean we can't start building a circumstantial case. Who knows? Maybe it'll even be enough to scare Lavon into a confession."

"Or maybe your rash actions for swift justice will result in a lawsuit against us as well as charges of tainting the evidence."

Harlan stared, dumbfounded. J.D. had been his mentor, had been grooming him to take over as sheriff and now he treated him like this? He'd done nothing wrong. Harlan's conscience was crystal clear. But there was no point in continuing the discussion.

"And if I refuse to leave work?" Harlan asked.

J.D. stood, hitching up his belt. "Son, you don't want to cross me. Get your ass out of here, think the situation over and we'll talk next week."

Harlan went to the door and then turned. "Why are you so afraid of Thaddeus Tedder?"

"I'm not." J.D. sat down and pulled a stack of papers toward him.

"Has he got some kind of hold over you?" Harlan asked quietly. Maybe Lilah was right. Maybe her uncle did pay J.D. for favors. It could have started years ago if Thaddeus had caught J.D. in a moment of weakness, and then his boss had been sucked into staying on the take.

"If you're in hot water with the Tedders, I can help you," Harlan offered.

J.D. nailed him with a glare. "What makes you say that?"

"You were recently seen accepting money from Thad."

J.D.'s hands slammed on the desk. "That's a damn lie. You got proof?"

"Not yet."

Harlan softly closed the door. Let his boss stew on that one.

Zelda scurried toward him with an empty cardboard box. "Thought you might need to pack up a few things," she said sympathetically, trying to push the box into his hands.

All eyes from the dozen or so cubicles were on him. So they'd heard J.D.'s rant.

He shook his head. "I don't need that box. I'll only be a gone a week. I'm coming back."

At least, he hoped so. No telling what kind of trick J.D. might have up his sleeve. Back in his office, he collected a few odds and ends, preparing to leave.

Wait. Not so fast. Just how crooked was his boss? Last time J.D. had been in his office, he'd disapproved of his reviewing the old Hilltop Strangler case and had taken Lilah's leather bracelet. On a hunch, Harlan looked up the number to the forensics office in Atlanta. If there was to be any progress on the case, he'd have to push it. Wouldn't hurt to prod one of his old friends and see if they could prioritize examining the bracelet. J.D. was already ticked off with him, so why not? He punched in the number and spoke to Doug almost at once. At least luck was with him on this.

But the news he received was a bombshell.

The bracelet had never been sent.

WAIT UNTIL UNCLE JASPER lit his eyes on this. Lilah kept a hand on top of the covered casserole dish as she swung into the potholed slash of dirt that passed for his driveway.

Jasper looked up, frowning, from where he was hoeing the vegetable garden. When he recognized his visitor, he nodded and walked to the house, laying the hoe alongside its exterior wall.

Lilah got out of the vehicle, holding up the covered dish. "A chicken and biscuit cobbler. Your favorite."

"It ain't my birthday. What's the occasion?"

"Just my way of saying thanks. If you hadn't directed the search team to the cave, I might have ended up spending the night in it."

He shrugged it off, as she knew he would. "Anyone would have done the same. That dish will do right nice. I'll slice up some fresh tomatoes and cucumbers to go with it."

"Which reminds me…" She laid the dish on the car's hood and opened the back door. "I told Harlan I was coming so he sent a few pepper plants by me to replace the ones he ran over the other day."

"Man made good on his promise, then."

"You can always count on Harlan." She transferred the plants into his thin weathered hands. He was too lean, she decided. The fattening casserole would do him good. She should start doing this once a week to make sure he put some meat on his bones.

"You go on in. I'm gonna pick us some fresh vegetables and water these here plants. They look a little peaked."

"Don't be too long," she said with a smile. "I'm hungry."

It seemed like she stayed that way these days. Lilah marched up the porch steps, careful not to bump into the crates and other junk her uncle insisted on keeping. She itched to pile it all in the front yard and burn it, but Jasper would never forgive her.

Truthfully, the inside of his place was almost as cluttered. He never threw anything away. Lilah placed the casserole on the table and then went to the den and sat on his old sofa. Dang, if she wasn't all tuckered out from working with Harlan this morning and then cooking. The events from yesterday must have been catching up to her body.

She kicked off her shoes and propped her feet on the coffee table, kicking aside a huge leather tome of some sort. Curious, she picked it up and riffled through it. A bible—should have guessed it. Uncle Jasper was devout, but in a hail-fire-and-brimstone kind of way that made her vaguely uncomfortable. Little slips of delicately aged

paper were stuck willy-nilly among the pages of King
James script. She took one out and read. "Everyone who
hates his brother is a murderer, and you know that no
murderer has eternal life present in him." 1 John 3:15.

And another: "Whoever brings ruin on their family
will inherit only wind, and the fool will be servant to
the wise." Proverbs 11:29.

Well, wasn't that just cheery. Carefully, she tucked
the paper slips back into their hidden homes. Whatever
her uncle chose to extrapolate from the bible was his
own business and reading his notes felt like a violation
of his privacy. So instead, Lilah flipped the pages to the
middle. Smack dab in the center, a long ancestry tree
lay folded accordion-style. Its pages were yellowed and
scribbled with Jasper's chicken-scratch handwriting.
Generations of Tedders were recorded, but she skipped
down to the latest entries. Her spirits took a nosedive at
the sight of her dad and sister's dates of death. One day
hers would be alongside them.

Enough with the gloomy thoughts. In a few months,
her baby's name would be listed as a birth on the family tree and that counted in the blessings column of life.
Her fingers traced over the names of great and great-great grandparents.

Ernest Tedder was a cruel man. Aunt Vi's words
popped into her mind and she searched for the man's
name. It was easy to spot. Amidst a sea of black and
blue ink, his name was recorded in crimson.

"Reading the Family Bible?"

She gasped and glanced up as Jasper stepped through

the screen door. "You scared me," she admitted with a slight laugh.

He slanted her an approving nod. "Does my heart proud to see a young'un reading the Holy Bible."

"I was just looking at our family tree," she admitted. "Can I ask you something, Uncle Jasper?"

"Reckon so." He settled cautiously into the chair across from her.

"I heard that your father was..." She hesitated. "A harsh man."

His ruddy face darkened. "Yer daddy tell you that?"

"It doesn't matter where I heard it." She glossed over his question. No sense getting him riled up at Aunt Vi. "Is it true?"

"Wicked." His thin lips clamped shut so tight they were white at the edges. "Despicable. Perverted."

Poor Uncle Jasper. It was obvious he'd suffered.

"Was Dad mistreated, too?" She had to know.

"Not so much. He was the baby. Thad and I were the ones that bore the brunt of his wrath."

He stared into space, apparently lost in painful memories.

"Would it help to talk about it?" she asked gently.

"Nope."

Now or never—she had one last question on the subject. "I heard he died in a hunting accident."

His eyes snapped to her. "What about it?"

"Was it really an accident?"

Silence roared in her ears, heavy and dreadful.

"Some have their suspicions," he answered at last.

With that open-ended response, she did have one more question left. "What do *you* think?"

"Sins of the father repeat from one generation to the next. Beware, Lilah. I'd hate to see anything happen to you."

He stood. "And that's all I have to say on the matter. Ever. Understood?"

When Uncle Jasper made up his mind, that was that.

"Yes, sir."

"Very well. Let's enjoy that meal you prepared."

But all through the midday meal and during the drive home, she replayed his cryptic remarks about the sins of the fathers repeating themselves through the generations.

All the way down to Cousin Lavon, who no doubt picked them up from his father. The gloom-and-doom path led her to even wilder imaginings. Uncle Jasper believed they were cursed. Intellectually, she knew there was no such thing but she couldn't shake the ugly questions and insinuations.

She was a Tedder. And it certainly seemed as if her family was cursed. First, Dad was killed and then Darla met the same fate. Who was next? And by whose hands?

It wasn't until later that evening, when she was drifting to sleep, that what had bothered her most of all that afternoon—that had been niggling in her subconscious for hours—made her sit bolt upright.

Just like Ernest Tedder's entry in the Family Bible, Dad and Darla's names had also been penned in crimson ink.

Chapter Thirteen

"He did *what*?" Lilah asked, nearly dropping the pan of water she had been setting on the stove.

Harlan took a seat at the table and ran a hand through his still-wet-from-the-shower hair. He'd debated not telling her what had happened, but she was bound to find out anyway. Besides, the lie of omission had sat heavily on him last night. He'd stayed out late at the bar with Sammy and Alvin, who'd insisted on buying him a couple of drinks and commiserating with him about his enforced leave of absence. When he'd finally returned home, Lilah had been fast asleep in front of the TV and he'd gently carried her to bed.

He'd reconciled himself to her deception and neither of them had spoken of it again. It was his baby after all and their futures were tied. But their relationship still seemed fragile, and he had to concede his own part in that.

"J.D. put me on administrative leave for a week. I'm not going to work this morning."

"That's so unfair. I shouldn't have insisted on going to the cave with you yesterday—"

"It was my decision," Harlan said firmly. She had enough worries without shouldering blame for his career hiccup. "And it was a culmination of several issues that have been brewing between us."

"Still." She set the pan on the stove and brought him a cup of coffee before sitting across from him at the kitchen table. "I've caused you nothing but trouble since I came home. I should leave."

"Don't you dare." That would be what finally did him in.

"What are you going to do?" she asked. "Return to work next week and hope J.D.'s cooled off?"

"No." He hadn't realized he'd already decided until that very moment. "I won't work for him again. Going back would feel like complicity in his crooked games. I won't be a part of it."

"Now you believe me when I say he's been on the take?"

"Should have from the start."

"If you don't go back, what are you going to do, then?" She hesitated, smoothing her hands over her jeans. "I have a little money saved, plus I might get a portion of that money Dad had socked away."

"I've got money," he said gruffly. "Not a problem."

"And I have health insurance with my job," she continued, eyes clouded with uncertainty. "That should cover most of my childbirth expenses. So I can certainly help there."

The baby. J.D.'s timing was lousy.

"Stop worrying. I'm fine," he said, reasoning out the possibilities. "I have plenty of contacts with other law enforcement agencies. I'll take a temporary position elsewhere and, hopefully, I'll win the sheriff's election."

"Doesn't seem right, though, that J.D.'s such a crook and gets to ride out his time until retirement."

"No free rides."

She cocked her head to the side. "What do you mean?"

"I believe J.D. might be the mole in the sheriff's office. The one that tips off the drug distributors before every raid that leads to a dead end. And I intend to find out the truth."

"How can you prove it?"

"I'm going to the state and federal people to tell them my suspicions. Convince them to set up a new raid bypassing J.D. and his entire office."

"That would be epic. But there's no telling how many people J.D. has under his influence," she warned. "Could be hard to get anything past him."

"His luck has to run out sometime," Harlan muttered, stirring sugar in his coffee.

She gave a sigh. "Suppose so."

"You don't sound convinced."

"It's just that… I wonder how this will affect my family. I don't want to believe Uncle Thad's involved with a drug ring, but if he is, Aunt Vi and his kids will be devastated at the news." She brought a hand to her mouth. "Oh, no. What about Ed? If he's in it, my nephews will suffer. If Ed goes to prison, they won't have a mother or a father."

He took her hand in his. "Let's agree to handle only one problem at a time. Deal?"

She drew a shaky breath. "Deal."

"How did your afternoon with Jasper go yesterday?" he asked, wanting to distract her from their problems.

"Unnerving."

"Oh?" He leaned back in his chair and sipped his coffee. "Jasper not his usual sociable self?" he joked.

Lilah snickered. "Right. Anyway, we got to talking about his father—my grandfather, Ernest. Jasper. He started going off the deep end talking about the sins of the fathers visited on the children, et cetera. So I asked him about the hunting accident, the one Aunt Vi said wasn't really an accident."

Harlan sat up straighter, pulse racing. "And?"

"He didn't come right out and say it, but he insinuated it wasn't an accident."

"I'll take a look at that old file, see what the official report says."

"Can't do that now can you?"

"I'll get Sammy to scan it and send me an email copy."

He'd also ask Sammy to check the evidence room and see if the leather bracelet was still there. Much as he mistrusted J.D., it was possible he'd locked it in storage and had forgotten about it.

Harlan took one last sip of his coffee and rose. "Let's go out for breakfast. It'll do us both good to get out of here."

"You sure? I've already started cooking."

"Save it for tomorrow."

She shrugged. "Suits me. I'll grab my purse."

That was one of the many things he liked about Lilah. She wasn't some glamour girl who would waste thirty minutes on hair and makeup. In less than five minutes, they were in her car and pulling out of the driveway. She'd insisted on driving, saying after the kind of day he'd suffered, he needed to relax and be chauffeured.

"Where are we going?" she asked, easing onto the county road.

"I could use a steak and—whoa!—slow down around that curve!"

Her compact car whipped around it way too fast for his comfort.

"Harlan—I can't!" Her voice rose several octaves. "The brakes aren't working!"

What the hell? He unbuckled his seat belt, practically crawled into her lap and pressed his left foot on top of hers. The brakes pounded to the floorboard, but the car didn't slow one iota.

They gathered speed as the car plummeted downhill. Trees flashed by the windows at tornado-level speed. *Damn.* He thought fast, scooting back to the passenger side. "It's okay, Lilah, keep steering. After the next curve, we'll come to a field. Make a sharp right into it when I give you the word."

The Mothershed's cow pasture was fairly level and, with luck, the car would grind to a stop with no harm to Lilah.

They rounded the curve.

"Now!" he yelled.

Lilah jerked the steering wheel to the right. Her car careened on its right side, and then fell back down to the ground on the opposite side with a crash of metal and broken glass. He tried gripping the dashboard, but his body toppled forward and his head hit something hard and unyielding. Pain exploded behind his eyes and then, mercifully, a black abyss of nothingness descended.

LILAH BLINKED. HOW ODD. She was in her car, but it wasn't moving. And she was parked in a field, with not a road in sight. The front windshield was cracked, and through the spider-webbed fissures, a cow chewed a mouthful of grass and stared at her indifferently.

Her hands hurt. Frowning, Lilah looked down and saw they were scratched and bloody. Cuts tattooed their backsides and spread up her wrists and forearms. How had that happened? She turned her head to the side and reality and remembrance slammed into her gut.

The brakes had failed and she'd wrecked. Harlan lay lifeless, and a deep gash on his forehead oozed blood.

He was hurt. Was he…?

"Oh, God, Harlan! Wake up. Please, wake up!"

Lilah leaned over and placed a hand over his heart. It beat.

"Hey, in there? Are y'all hurt?"

Outside, a man and a woman ran to the car. The man struggled, but managed to open the door on her side. Arms lifted her out of the vehicle. "No," she protested. She didn't want to leave Harlan's side. "Help Harlan. Please."

Strong arms placed her carefully on the ground and then the woman loomed overhead, her eyes wide with pity. She pushed a lock of hair from Lilah's face. "We will, sugar. Don't you fret now. We called for help."

In no time, a siren's wail erupted and it seemed people

were everywhere. She struggled to get a glimpse of Harlan, finally spotting him being helped onto a stretcher and into a waiting ambulance. EMTs brought one to her and she was lifted and placed in the ambulance beside Harlan.

The shock started to wear off, and self-reproach set in. "What have I done?" she sobbed and turned her head to face Harlan—whose eyes were open.

He reached out a hand and squeezed hers. "You okay?" he asked.

"Yes. But you…" Her throat closed up.

"I'm fine." He managed a slight smile. "Might have a headache a day or two, but no big deal."

She let out a sound that was halfway between a sob and a laugh.

"The baby?" he asked hoarsely. "Everything okay?"

She squeezed his hand this time. "I think so. They can check at the hospital."

Unbidden tears streamed down her cheeks. This was all her fault somehow. It was her car and she'd been driving. "I don't know what happened. The brakes were fine earlier. I promise."

"Don't cry. I believe you. I suspect someone cut the brake line."

"Who? Why?" Damn, she was sick of this nightmare.

"I don't know yet, but I'll find out. I promise you that."

"I want it to stop. I want…" She wanted to leave. Pack up and move as far away from here as soon as possible. Mom had been right to run away all those years ago.

Ran and never looked back, never returned. Not even for her ex-husband's funeral.

Lilah laid a hand over her eyes, remembering all the reasons she'd stayed away from Lavender Mountain. There was nothing for her here but heartbreak.

... ...
... ...
... ...

Chapter Fourteen

Lilah lay in the early morning darkness, hands over her belly. She stared out the bedroom window, debating her options and her timing as the sun rose, casting violet and purple splashes on the horizon. Nowhere was as hauntingly beautiful or as deadly as home. No matter how long or how far she roamed, this place was forever rooted in her soul.

The ultrasound had checked out normal—the baby was safe. A small miracle that she intended to honor by taking every precaution possible to avoid danger, no matter the sacrifice. And that meant leaving Lavender Mountain for good, Harlan or no Harlan. Much as she loved him, she couldn't put their child's life in danger.

He tossed in bed beside her, moaning softly. She ran a hand over his back, loving the feel of his smooth lean muscles. Lilah's heart squeezed at the idea of saying goodbye. How dangerous could it be to wait a few days—make sure he was over the worst of the concussion?

No. The longer she waited, the harder it would be. If she was lucky, and if Harlan truly loved her, he'd listen to reason and agree to go with her. Start over somewhere safer and with more opportunity for both of them.

"Harlan?" she whispered.

He rolled over at once and opened his eyes, instantly alert.

"Want me to get you a pain pill?"

He sat halfway up and leaned against a bank of pillows. "No. I need a clear head and have too much to do."

"You're off this week. Remember? Courtesy of J.D. Stay in bed and heal. You've got a nasty concussion."

"That might also be courtesy of J.D."

"Really?" She leaned over him. "It was my car. Seems more likely that whoever did this was after me, not you."

"If they hurt you, they hurt me. Either way, it's a message."

"But what message? And who sent it? None of this makes sense."

"Could have been J.D. trying to warn or silence me. I came too close to finding out the truth about him and shutting down his gravy train."

"Or it could be the Hillside Strangler who believes I have his bracelet and wants it back at any cost," she countered.

Harlan flung off the covers and swung his legs over the side of the bed, pausing to draw a ragged breath.

"You're getting up?"

"I'm calling Lewis Slidell in the state investigator's office. Tell him my suspicions about what's going on up here."

"Think he'll listen?"

He flashed a wan smile. "I see you share the Tedder faith in law enforcement."

"Can hardly blame me for that. Guess while you're handling your business, I'll deal with the insurance company about getting my car fixed. My favorite thing to do," she said with a groan.

Lilah carefully eased out of bed, wincing at the sore muscles in her back and legs.

Harlan frowned. "You're hurting."

"A little. No pain pills for me, though. Not even over-the-counter stuff."

"You stay in bed and I'll bring you breakfast."

"I'm not the one with a concussion." He opened his mouth to protest, and she cut him off. "Let's compromise. We'll make toast and coffee together."

"Deal." He stood, grimacing for a moment before following her slow progress to the kitchen. She flipped on lights in the hallway and the kitchen.

"If you'll start the coffee, I'm going to check the newspaper," he said. "See if there's been any press on the so-called accident."

"You think there will be?"

"I gave a statement to the police. Told them what to look for in the car." He gave a sly grin. "And it's entirely possible that the reporter from the local paper was in hearing range when I said it."

"Nice," she said with an answering smile. "They'll know you're onto them."

She measured out coffee grinds and was about to pour them in the pot when Harlan slammed the door and marched into the kitchen waving the newspaper like a machine. "J.D. sure didn't waste any time kicking me to the curb."

He unfurled the rolled-up paper and handed it to her. *Sheriff J.D. Bentley endorses Officer Alvin Lee in Upcoming Election.*

Lilah's mouth opened in a round *o* of astonishment. "How could he?" She burned with indignation on Harlan's behalf.

He flung the paper in the wastebasket. "If Alvin gets elected, I have a feeling it's just going to be more of the same here in Elmore County. He's a miniature J.D."

She gave a long sigh. "Bet you're sorry now I ever came back here."

"Course not, Lilah. This has nothing to do with you and everything to do with me getting too close to J.D.'s illegal crap."

"You know, this might be a good thing," she said slowly.

"The hell?" Harlan scowled, the stitches in his forehead twisting ominously, looking ready to come undone.

"If you don't run for sheriff—"

"Oh, I'm running," he cut in, the muscles in his jaw twitched.

"Forget the race."

His incredulous gaze almost undermined her courage. "Look, I wasn't going to say anything for a few days. Was going to make sure you were okay first, get a rental car and—"

"I'm fine and you can use my car or we can get you a rental today. So whatever it is, spit it out."

"Fine," she snapped. "That's what I was trying to do."

Harlan folded his arms and sat down at the table. "I have a feeling this is bad news. Go ahead."

The man wasn't going to make this easy. Best to spill it all at once.

"I'm leaving," she announced.

"Leaving…what?" His mulish stance was replaced with a look of confusion.

"This place."

"You're leaving *me*?"

"Lavender Mountain. Not you."

"Same thing."

"It's not. Don't you see? Maybe this was meant to be. We can make a break and leave together. What's to stop us?" Doubt assailed her. "That is…if you still want me."

"I want you," he insisted.

"Really? You once let a scumbag like J.D. ruin everything because of your ambition. Sounds to me like you're doing the same thing again by staying here instead of leaving with me."

"That's not fair. You know why I want to be sheriff."

"How bad do you want that career advancement, Harlan? More than you want me and the baby?"

There she'd said it. What she'd promised herself she would never ever do. She'd just forced Harlan's hand to choose between her and his career.

"Don't back me into a corner."

"Don't tell me what I can and can't do," she retorted. This wasn't how she imagined this discussion going down. If she wanted a calm exchange, it had to start with her. Lilah sat down at the opposite end of the table.

"I was going to wait before I brought this up, but now that it's out, let's see it through. I don't want my baby—"

"*Our* baby."

"Okay, I don't want to raise our baby here. I don't want Lavon anywhere near my—I mean, our—child. I don't want our kid growing up alongside moonshiners, alcoholics and drug dealers."

"Be reasonable, Lilah. Drugs are everywhere."

She ignored that. "I'm going to raise him—or her— somewhere less violent. A town where his name won't be associated with crime. I grew up with that stigma and I don't want our kid to go through the same."

"The kid won't have your name, he'll have mine."

As if that mattered. Everyone knew everyone here, along with everyone's family history. "And I won't let Uncle Thad and my cousins set a poor example of how to live."

"Thought you loved your family."

"I do. But I want better for our child. I won't have one of mine going through what I've been through with two close family members murdered."

"I'll protect you both."

"You can't. I think the car wreck proved that."

"Don't you see? That's why I want to be sheriff, to end all the liquor and drug running and violence. I can do it, too."

"Good luck with that," she scoffed.

"Have a little faith in me."

"Lavender Mountain has a way of corrupting even the best of folks."

"Not me. You were born and raised here and you turned out just fine."

"Have I?"

"What kind of a dumb question is that?"

Wrong thing to say. He could have said, *I think you're wonderful.* Or, *I love you.* Or better, *Let's go down to the justice of the peace right now and get married.*

But he hadn't, and she had her answer. No matter that she'd gone to college and had managed her life as a decent law-abiding and tax-paying citizen—once a Tedder, always a Tedder. Deep down, Harlan didn't believe she was good enough to be his wife.

Her face flamed. Uncle Jasper was right. This was playing house and she was done with childhood games.

She slowly rose from the table. "I think we're done here."

"What does that mean?" he asked as she sauntered out of the room and down the hall. "We haven't finished talking this out yet."

Lilah went to the bedroom and dragged the suitcase out from under the bed. First, she dumped the contents of her lingerie drawer in it and then opened the second drawer of the dresser.

"You're leaving me? Now?"

"Yes," she answered, not looking at him. "Maybe without me dragging you down, you'll win your precious election."

"Look at me, Lilah."

She lifted her chin and leveled a stare. Harlan leaned against the doorjamb looking strong and as sexy as ever. The stitches on his forehead did nothing to detract from his appeal. If anything, it added a devastating touch of vulnerability.

"So you expect me to drive you to your apartment?

Aid and abet you in this mess?" he asked with a cool trace of amusement in his tone. "Seeing as you don't have a car right now."

Oh, yeah. She'd forgotten about that little matter. Lilah cleared her throat, gathering her dignity. "A ride to the rent-a-car place will suffice. But if that's too much trouble, I can call Uncle Jasper."

He strolled over and placed a hand on the small of her back, just above her hips. "Lilah," he said softly. "Don't go."

"Why should I stay?" Lilah's voice was tiny and wobbly, even to her own ears. Even more to her chagrin, she was near tears. She'd cried more these past few weeks than she'd cried in her entire life and it frustrated her. Those pregnancy hormones were doing a real number on her emotions.

"Because I want you," Harlan said. "Hell, because I *need* you. At least stay here until I catch the killer. If not for me, for the baby."

She dropped the T-shirt she'd been folding. "Not fair to spring the baby on me."

"Whatever it takes to get you to stay."

"I should be okay at my apartment."

He quirked a brow. "After your neighbor reported seeing a man creeping around there? Doesn't sound safe to me."

"Oh, *all right*," she conceded ungraciously. "I'll stay, with one stipulation."

"Anything."

"I go back to the spare bedroom."

He sucked in his breath, as if she'd dealt him a low blow. "Why? Still mad at me?"

Not angry—she was hurt. Because Harlan didn't love her. He found her lacking as a suitable wife. Prolonging their affair would only make it harder to bear once it was over. Lilah bit her tongue, though. She wouldn't let him know how much that hurt.

"Damn right, I'm still mad at you," she lied.

He took her hand. "C'mon, time for a truce. We'll eat breakfast and I'll drink my morning cup of coffee. We're both sore from the wreck and grouchy as bears this morning."

She took the olive branch. It would make life easier to be on amicable terms with Harlan for the remainder of her stay.

"I won't say no to a couple pieces of toast."

"Toast? I'm going to make us a *real* breakfast—biscuits, gravy, bacon and eggs. You go on back to bed and I'll wake you when it's ready."

She eyed the bed longingly. "I am tired," she admitted. She'd gotten up too early, still tense over the car wreck. They both could have been killed so easily. She gave an involuntary shudder.

Harlan returned her suitcase under the bed and folded down the bedspread. She slipped back into the warm cotton that smelled of Harlan's masculine scent, and he pulled the sheets over her, tucking her in like a child.

"Sweet dreams, honey," he said, planting a swift kiss on her forehead.

Lilah closed her eyes and curled against the pillows. Small wonder she loved him. But sometimes, love wasn't enough.

Chapter Fifteen

This was going to be awkward.

Harlan tucked the padded envelope under his right arm and squared his shoulders. He had nothing to be ashamed of. Resolutely, he pushed open the door to the sheriff's office and entered.

Sammy rose from his desk at once and came to greet him. "Hey, Harlan. Man, you're gonna be left with an ugly scar on your forehead. Got something for us?"

He followed Sammy into his old office, past the gaze of curious, but still friendly, former coworkers. Only Alvin turned a cold shoulder. No surprise there.

"You sure J.D. is out for the day?" Harlan asked, closing the door.

"Positive. That psychological profile training is scheduled for two days. It'll be late by the time he drives back from Atlanta tomorrow evening." Sammy nodded at the package. "Picked that up from the mechanics?"

"Yep. One cut brake line. Got his expert opinion on that recorded on a signed statement. Said no one else had touched the auto part but him."

"Knew you'd cross your t's and dot your i's," Sammy said. "You always do. Everyone here knows it, too."

"Except Alvin," Harlan muttered. But he appreciated the show of support.

"Alvin's an ass."

"Not going to argue about that. Do you have a copy of the old Ernest Tedder hunting accident?"

Sammy slid a few papers across the desk. "Already printed it out in case J.D. made a bitch move and disabled your computer access. Not much in that old report that I can see. Back then, you basically just had a coroner's report and an officer statement."

Harlan scanned the thin account. Ernest Tedder was shot once in the back with his own rifle. His son Jasper had borrowed the gun to go hunting, and had mistakenly shot Ernest only a quarter mile from their family home early one January morning. Witnesses stated that Jasper, then only sixteen years old, was devastated. The family filed no charges, and the coroner's report stated that Ernest died almost immediately when the lone bullet pierced his heart and lungs.

"Shot in the back just like Chauncey and Darla," Harlan mused aloud.

"You still trying to find a connection between the three Tedder murders?" Sammy asked. "Maybe you could argue the last two are, but you're stretching with this old one."

"Surprised I never heard of this before about Jasper accidentally shooting his father."

"Eh, well, it's ancient history. Poor kid. He must have felt awful. No wonder he grew up to be such a crackpot."

Harlan glanced at the second page of the report and observed that it was signed by Investigating Officer J.D. Bentley. Seemed noteworthy enough that J.D. could have at least mentioned the old case while they searched for Chauncey and Darla's murderer.

"Anything new on the recent Tedder murders?" Harlan asked.

"Not a thing. Alvin's still leaning on Ed, trying to force a confession, but I have my doubts the guy offed his wife."

"Lilah doesn't believe Ed did it, either. I'm inclined to agree."

This was the case that most disturbed him. Chauncey hadn't had much time left in his natural life before it was cut short, and he'd had any number of people angry with him at any given time. But Darla was different. She'd left behind three young sons, and there was no apparent reason someone would want her dead, unless you believed it was the result of a domestic dispute. Hard to believe she had been killed over her wedding ring and a few pieces of costume jewelry.

But they weren't just any old costume jewelry pieces. They specifically belonged to two prior homicide victims murdered over twenty years ago.

There was a connection between all five murders, Harlan felt sure of it. And Lilah could have so easily been the sixth victim. Bile rose at the back of his throat. He couldn't lose her. Even the thought of her leaving Lavender Mountain again made him sick. Somehow, he'd find a way to convince her to stay. For now, he needed to concentrate on keeping her alive.

"Our best hope of solving these cases is if there's a fingerprint on the leather bracelet Lilah found."

Sammy glumly agreed. "But the forensics lab takes forever, and there's probably too many prints on it to get any clear markings."

"That's another reason I came in today," Harlan said. "J.D. never mailed the bracelet to the lab. I need to get it out."

"Why would he sit on it?" Sammy asked, lips curling in disgust. "He knows how hard we've been working to solve this. We've pursued every clue with no luck yet."

"That's about to change."

Sammy leaned forward, eyes lit with anticipation. "What's up?"

"After I have Zelda log the brake-line package into the evidence log, I'm going to personally deliver it, and the leather bracelet, to the lab in Atlanta. I've already called Doug and he's expecting me."

Sammy let out a low whistle. "How do you plan on sneaking past the dragon lady? She keeps that evidence room key under close guard."

"I'll sweet talk her, bribe her—whatever it takes."

"Good luck with that," he said with a snort.

"If all else fails—the woman has to take a bathroom break sometime, right? And I know where she keeps the key."

"J.D. will have a fit when he finds out." Sammy's forehead creased in concern. "You do this and J.D. will make your life hell. That's *if* he doesn't fire you."

"He won't fire me."

"The hell he won't—"

"Because I'm quitting." Harlan lifted a sealed envelope he'd brought in with the brake-line package. "Here's my letter of resignation. Signed, sealed and about to be delivered."

"Oh, man. Don't do that! The election's around the corner and I think you can still win. Everyone knows Alvin's unfit, even if J.D. did endorse his sorry ass."

"I said I'm quitting this job, not that I'm dropping out of the race."

"But… You think that's wise? I mean, given that Lilah's expectin'."

"I've lined up an interview for a temporary job." Harlan hesitated, then decided it wouldn't hurt to tell Sammy his plans. "That's another reason I'm driving to Atlanta. The guys at the state troopers headquarters have been trying to recruit me for over a year. I called and told them I was available and they wanted to talk to me right away."

Sammy shook his head and ran a hand through his dark close-cropped hair. "I'm glad for you, of course, but you'll sure be missed 'round here. We've worked together a long time."

"Hopefully, I won't be away but a few months." Harlan grinned at his old friend. "And when I return, it will be as your new boss."

"Glad to stay on your good side, then." Sammy cocked his head at the closed door. "Got the feeling old Alvin isn't too happy with me right now, consorting with the enemy as it were."

"Screw Alvin." He rose from his chair. "Now to charm that evidence key out of Zelda's tight-fisted hands."

"Good luck."

"Go back to your desk and steer clear of what I'm about to do. No sense getting yourself in hot water. Far as anyone knows, you and I have just been in here shootin' the breeze."

Sammy rose and shook his hand. "Here's to solving those cases."

Harlan waited a couple of minutes after Sammy left, then picked up his items and headed for Zelda's desk.

She was there, manning the fort as usual. Would have been too much to hope she and J.D. were both gone for the day.

"Hello, gorgeous," he said, taking a seat by her desk. An online crossword puzzle showed on her computer monitor.

"What's a four-letter word for a legendary story?" she asked, not bothering to look up. "Starts with an *m*."

"Myth."

Zelda typed it in and pushed up her bifocals. "Yep, that'll do it. What are you doing here, Harlan? Boss told you to take off."

"Being the excellent employee I am, I couldn't stay away."

He ignored her snort.

"I'm not staying long. Just want you to enter this package on the evidence log." He laid the bundle on her desk.

Sighing, she opened the front drawer and pulled out a hardbound notebook, riffling through to the current page. "Here you go."

Harlan entered his name, date and time, and type of

evidence. Zelda's eyes were slanted toward his entry and he stifled a smile. The indifferent air was an act. She wanted to know everything that went down in the office.

He snapped the notebook shut and handed it back to her.

"Brake line, huh?" Her gray eyes zeroed in on his forehead. "You look awful. Glad you're okay."

"I'm touched." He gave her a wink. "Didn't know you cared."

"That so? What are you buttering me up for?"

He feigned innocence. "I'm not. Why don't you give me the key and I'll put this up while you finish your puzzle."

"I'm the only one who goes in there. You know that."

"Can you make an exception? Just this once?"

Zelda tapped a finger to her lips, considering. "Why you so anxious to do it yourself? Never cared before."

To hell with charm, maybe honesty would do the trick. "I've never had anyone try to kill me before. Would ease my mind to see this package locked up."

"Newspaper said it was Lilah's car that wrecked."

"Would have been more awful if she'd been killed instead of me. Or lost our baby."

Zelda grimaced and a lone tear ran down her cheek.

What was this? He'd seen her examine the goriest crime photos and bloodied weapons with nary a hitch.

"I forgot about the baby," she said hoarsely.

Then he remembered. Over twenty years ago, Zelda's two-year-old grandson had died in a car accident. Even after all these years, she must keep his memory close to the heart. Sometimes he forgot that even the gruffest people in his line of work harbored heartaches just like anyone else. Everyone had vulnerabilities.

Zelda pulled a keychain out of her purse and handed it to him. There was only one key on it. "You do what you have to do." She cleared her throat and turned back to the computer. "Now let me get back to my puzzle."

"Yes ma'am."

He debated touching her arm, but Zelda would probably rather he forget he even witnessed her moment of softness.

Once in the evidence room, he haphazardly tossed the package on the nearest shelf. The real cut brake line from Lilah's car was safely locked up in his own vehicle. He'd pass it on to Doug to check for fingerprints, along with that leather bracelet—if he could find it. When he'd signed Zelda's log, he'd peeked at the other entries, and there was no note of a bracelet.

He went to the shelf marked for the current year and month and scanned it. There was a sealed bag of Chauncey's clothes he'd worn the day he was shot, next to it was a similar bag for Darla's clothes, and a couple of ominous looking tagged knives seized in an assault.

But no bracelet.

He checked again. Then carefully examined other nearby shelves to see if it had been misplaced.

Nothing.

Damn J.D. What had he done with it? Why didn't he want it examined? Despite the humidity in the small cramped room, his skin prickled with uneasiness. Perhaps J.D. was involved in more than covering up moonshine and drug operations. If so, trying to solve these cases would be a bigger challenge than he'd imagined.

Harlan locked up the room and returned to Zelda's desk where a scowling Alvin waited.

"What were you doing in there?" Alvin asked, a waspish edge to his voice.

"Depositing the latest evidence in a case. Who are you to question me?"

Alvin puffed out his chest. "I'm going to be your boss in a few months, unless J.D. fires you first."

"That's not going to happen." Harlan handed Zelda the sealed envelope. "My letter of resignation," he told her. "Effective immediately."

Alvin's jaw slackened for a moment and then he bestowed a smug grin. "Wise decision. Now I suggest you leave. You have no business here."

He pasted a smile on his face. "That's okay. I got what I wanted. Take care, Zelda."

Alvin barely moved enough to get out of his way, and Harlan brushed shoulders with him. He'd never cared much for the guy, but now he'd be impossible to work with.

As he neared the exit, he felt a tap on his shoulder.

"I'll hold on to the letter a few days," Zelda said. "In case you change your mind."

Who knew the dragon lady was such a softie? "I won't, but thanks."

Harlan pushed open the door and walked into sunshine, feeling lighter. This was the right thing to do. Tension had been building between him and J.D. for months and he didn't realize how oppressive it had become until resigning. With any luck, he'd have a new job by the end of the day, and new leads on the murders.

"Ouch." Lilah yanked her hand back and frowned at the stinging nettles. "I've got something for you," she muttered. "A good vinegar dousing."

She stood and stretched. After the heat of the afternoon sun had passed, she'd decided to get some fresh air. It had felt good to weed Harlan's neglected vegetable patch. Nothing like digging in the dirt to keep her problems at bay. With the exception of the occasional passing vehicle and the sound of the radio from the open living room window, it had been a quiet and productive time.

Lilah started for the house. After soaking the nettles in vinegar, she'd take a nice long bath and then read in bed. Since Harlan was going to grab supper on the road driving back from Atlanta, she'd forego cooking and enjoy a sandwich.

A light flickered. In the deepening twilight, the silhouette of a man walked by the lamp near the couch. Heart clamoring, she climbed down the porch step and flattened her body against the exterior wall. Had he seen her?

The sound of a drawer being jerked open drifted through the screen window. Luckily, he appeared too absorbed in his search to have noticed her. Was he looking for valuables? If so, the thief was plum out of luck. Harlan didn't keep large amounts of cash lying around.

Her mind raced with questions. Who was it? How had he entered the house without her hearing? True, she hadn't locked the doors, but it had seemed like she would have seen or heard something.

Whoever it was, he was way too thin to be Harlan. Besides, she'd have noticed him pulling his car in the driveway.

Lilah swiftly debated her options. Her only set of car keys—along with her cell phone—were on the kitchen counter. Escaping to the car or calling for help was a no-go. The nearest neighbor was a mile away. Her gaze traveled to the tree line at the side of Harlan's property. She could hide there until either the person left or Harlan returned.

But first, she'd have to take a risk and run across the yard. If he saw her…

But what other choice did she have? Wait here until he found her cowering near the window?

She ran, not daring to look back and see if she'd been discovered.

"Lilah? Are you out there?"

That voice again. The same one from the cave. She hit the tree line and scrabbled behind a large oak. One quick glimpse, she promised herself. Just to know if she'd been followed. Carefully, she peeked around the tree.

Lavon leaned out the window; some slight noise must have alerted him to her presence.

So it *was* her cousin after all. Had Lavon come by to rob them—or did he have a more sinister motive? Perhaps he thought no one was home, that she was out with Harlan or friends.

He was so busted this time.

Seconds later, the front door opened and slammed

shut. Lavon ran toward the road and she watched as he jogged around a bend and past her line of vision. He wasn't carrying anything in his hands that she could see. Was he crazy? More important, was he coming back?

A car roared to life, heading in the opposite direction of Harlan's house. Lavon must have parked his car down the road and walked here.

What a creep.

Lilah hightailed it back to the house and locked herself inside. Her breath was ragged and her heart scuttled like a frightened rabbit as she slammed down the open window and walked through all the rooms, ensuring all the other windows were down and locked, too. And she still didn't feel safe. In Harlan's closet, she grabbed the shotgun from the top shelf, pulled back the slide and checked the chamber.

Whew. Loaded.

She returned to the den and opened the desk drawer Lavon had been messing with. A quart-sized bag of marijuana, a small plastic baggie of white, powdered substance and three rolled joints laid inside. Lilah drew back, as if she'd discovered a coiled rattlesnake prepared to strike. These didn't belong to Harlan, no way. Lavon had put them there. Quickly, she opened all the other drawers, but nothing else had been tampered with.

How long had he been in the house before she'd noticed? It couldn't have been too long—she'd gone in for a glass of water about twenty minutes before spotting him. Still, that could have given him time to plant more drugs. Lilah went to the kitchen and opened cabinet drawers. Nothing there.

Just to be safe, she would check the bedrooms and bathrooms, too.

Elliptical beams of white light gashed through the front window, followed immediately by a strobing blue light. The angry crunch of gravel on the driveway sounded as harsh as a million firecrackers exploding.

Lilah went to the window and drew back the curtain an inch. J.D. and Alvin exited the sheriff's cruiser at the same time.

This was a set up.

Lilah picked up the cell phone on the end table, and then set it back down. No time to call Harlan.

She had all of two seconds to consider her limited options.

Decision made, Lilah grabbed the two baggies and the joints, and she ran to the bathroom. With trembling hands, she emptied the joints and the contents of the baggies into the toilet and flushed.

A pounding sounded from the front door. "Open up!" a voice ordered.

Marijuana buds and leaves still floated on top of the toilet water and she flushed again. Should she risk trying to flush the baggies, too, or would the toilet overrun? She'd rather have a plumbing crisis than a go-to-jail crisis, but an overrunning toilet would alert them to what she'd done.

She took the two baggies and quickly rinsed them in the sink, hoping that got rid of all traces.

"Open the door," the voice commanded again.

Lilah swiped at the inside of the wet baggies with a towel. She couldn't just throw them in the trash—

too obvious. She flung open the small toiletry cabinet, scanned its contents and then grabbed a box of tampons she'd purchased months ago and left there. Most men seemed to have an unreasonable aversion to female hygiene products, so perhaps stuffing the baggies full of tampons would keep them from examining them too closely.

She placed the baggies in the cabinet and shut the door. A quick glance at the toilet and she drew a deep breath. No residue, but she flushed it again for good measure. There—that was the best she could do. Feeling like a low-class criminal, she went to the front door toting a gun in one hand, cell phone in the other. Quickly, she pressed Harlan's number only to reach his voice mail. She left a terse message. "Get home quick. There's a drug bust and you've been framed."

Lilah jerked open the door.

J.D.'s face was stern, and Lilah involuntarily swallowed hard. Next to him, Alvin mimicked J.D.'s hard set to his mouth. What a pip-squeak.

J.D. thrust a paper at her midsection. "I have a subpoena to search this house for drugs and drug paraphernalia. Move aside, please."

She took a step back and let the paperwork fall to the floor. The sheriff walked in first with Alvin close behind.

"Where's Harlan?" J.D. asked.

"Be home any minute." At least, she hoped so.

"You take the kitchen and I'll start in this room," J.D. said, pointing at Alvin.

From the kitchen, she heard Alvin opening drawers

and cabinet doors. J.D. made a pretense of lifting sofa cushions and examining objects on the fireplace mantle. Only a matter of time before he went to the desk that straddled the den and the kitchen. Did Lavon have time to plant anything else? Surely the stuff he'd left was more than enough to get Harlan fired from any job in law enforcement—ever—and maybe even jail time. And he could just forget his dream of becoming sheriff.

Lilah picked up her cell phone and hit *record*.

"What are you doing there?" J.D. barked.

"Recording you. Just to keep everything on the up-and-up."

"Turn it off."

Lilah wasn't sure if she was within her rights to record the search, so she didn't argue. But the minute he turned his back to her, she again hit *record* and turned the cell phone face down on the couch. If she was lucky, maybe she'd at least have an audio recording if something crazy went down.

She watched him, clasping her shaking hands together. So, he and Lavon worked together. No wonder the police never found anything on a drug raid. J.D. made damn sure they were tipped-off. And now he wanted to set Harlan up to be arrested just to get him out of the way?

Her body shook violently, but this time with anger. And what would they do to her? Claim she was a drug dealer, too? Her gut churned as if a gallon of icy slush rolled inside. What could that mean for her baby if she was arrested? They might not let her keep the child.

Oh, hell no. She would fight them every step of the way.

J.D. lumbered toward the desk.

"Already sure you did a thorough search in this room?"

He swung around. "We can come back later with the narcotics dogs."

"No need. You already know exactly where to search."

"What's that supposed to mean?" J.D.'s eyes narrowed and his angry energy filled the room.

"It means you're about to be disappointed." Probably wasn't the smartest idea challenging J.D., yet she couldn't keep the words bottled. "But go on, search the desk. That's where you've been heading all along."

"How—" He snapped his mouth shut and glowered, face flushed.

Alvin hustled over from the kitchen. "What's that supposed to mean?"

"It means J.D. is one hundred percent positive there are drugs in that top right drawer of the desk."

Alvin glanced back and forth between them. "What am I missing here?"

J.D. swiveled, yanking out all the desk drawers, and then slowly turned to face her. "Go check the back of the house," he ordered Alvin, keeping his eyes trained on Lilah.

Alvin hesitated but obeyed.

"Looks like it's just you and me now," J.D. said darkly. He took a menacing step forward.

Lilah scrambled to her feet. "Alvin! Come help me."

J.D. froze.

Alvin rushed back to the den. "Now what?"

"The woman's getting hysterical, that's all. Find anything?"

"I just got started."

"Let's go. We'll deal with this another time."

Alvin's mouth dropped open. If she wasn't so furious, she might have found it comical. "Why? We haven't even begun a proper search."

Instead of bothering to answer, J.D. strode for the door. Lilah followed the men out, watching as they drove off into the night.

She might have won the battle, but this was far from over.

Chapter Sixteen

Finally, Harlan pulled in the driveway. No Lilah at the door welcoming him home, but at least J.D. wasn't there, either. He'd half-expected to find three or four sheriff's cars at the house with blue lights blazing.

"Lilah?" he called out, stepping through the front door. A small piece of paper was lying on the floor and he picked it up. A subpoena notice to search his premises for illegal substances. Harlan crumpled it in his hands and tossed it on the coffee table.

She emerged from the kitchen, clutching a giant bag of potato chips and a glass of soda. "Present and accounted for. I've been stress eating since they left," she added with a wan smile.

He sat on the sofa and patted the empty space beside him. "How about sharing those with me while you fill me in on everything."

She plopped down beside him. "I was outside weeding the garden until it grew dark. When I started back in the house, I saw Lavon through the window. He was rummaging inside, by the desk. I ran for the woods and waited for him to leave."

Bastard. His scalp prickled, imagining what Lavon might have done if Lilah hadn't spotted him and had walked into the house. "He didn't give chase?"

"No. He ran out the front door and then I heard him start his car down the road. I came back in and found bags of marijuana and cocaine, and a few rolled joints. J.D. arrived and pounded on the door for me to let him in." She gave a dispirited laugh. "So I did what any guilty druggie would do. I flushed it all down the toilet before opening the door. Did I do the right thing?"

"Absolutely. If you hadn't, I'd be in handcuffs right now, waiting for someone to set bail."

"You should have seen J.D.'s face when he searched the desk and nothing was there. At least, in the end, even Alvin looked at J.D. with suspicion."

"The little runt was with him. Shouldn't be surprised, I guess."

She shrugged and took a swallow from her glass. "I suspect Alvin's not totally corrupt. He acted as if he still had a conscience. What are you going to do now? They won't stop. Not until they have you—or me—behind bars."

"Not going to happen." He reached in the chip bag and started munching. "I spilled my guts out today with Lewis Slidell—laid out everything and my suspicions about J.D.'s involvement. He's putting together an emergency law enforcement raid. First thing in the morning, Lavender Mountain will be crawling with state troopers, GBI and FBI agents, and anyone else he can get together. They've wanted a break in this drug ring operation for years."

"It's bigger than that," Lilah said, slapping her hands on her thighs. "I don't care about the drug ring. I want to know who killed Dad and Darla, and why they're coming after me."

"Of course, that's my number one priority." He moved the bag of chips to the coffee table and took her hand. "I believe J.D. knows who the killer is, and he's being paid to keep his mouth shut. He's hindered the investigation of the old Hilltop Strangler cases, as well as your family's recent murders."

Harlan felt a tremor run through her small hand. He ran a finger along the throbbing vein in her wrist, painfully aware of how fragile and precious Lilah's life was. And his baby's, too. Whatever it took, they would solve these crimes and catch the killer.

"Is it possible J.D. is the killer?" she asked.

"I wouldn't rule it out."

"If Alvin hadn't been with him tonight... The way J.D. looked at me when I challenged him... I believe he might have hurt me."

Anger pulsed in his temples, a solar flare of energy and heat that radiated down his spine and pooled in his gut.

"Oh, I almost forgot." She rose, went to the desk and returned with her cell phone. "Not sure this can help you, but I have audio of what went down tonight. J.D. had a conniption fit when I tried to video the search, but I managed to record sound."

He took the phone and transferred the video to his email account. "I'll listen to it tomorrow with Lewis and everyone else. Every bit helps."

"Wish I could see J.D.'s face tomorrow when he comes in to work."

"I'm looking forward to it. Crooked cops are scum. When we get through this investigation, Elmore County will have the cleanest law enforcement staff in Georgia."

Lilah cocked her head to the side, studying him. He couldn't quite fathom the play of emotions in her gray eyes.

"I'm glad. You're going to be the best sheriff we've ever had."

"Lavender Mountain will be safe—a good area to live and raise kids. *Our* kids."

She moved to leave, but he gently tugged her arm, pulling her small body onto his lap. "I promise, it will be—and soon."

There was a gulf between them; the ugly words from yesterday hung in the air. Lilah had distanced herself from him—a lonely abyss he was desperate to bridge. He kissed her full lips, still salty from their shared snack.

Lilah moaned and their tongues met. He couldn't fathom how or why, but Lilah was so sweet and so damn sexy at the same time. He moved his hands under her T-shirt and glided them up the smooth contour of her hips and then the arch of her back.

"Stop."

Lilah scrabbled to her feet and ran a hand through her hair. "Not a good idea," she said in a shaky voice. "Nothing's changed."

"Everything's about to change," he argued.

"I'm still who I am."

"I've never asked you to be anything different." What

was she after? He scratched his head. "You're perfect just the way you are."

Pewter-gray eyes nailed him. "Do you love me?"

Did he? His heart quickened at the same moment his tongue stuck to the roof of his mouth. *Go on. Tell her what she wants to hear.* Trouble was, he didn't much believe in love. He'd certainly never witnessed it between his parents.

Harlan stared into Lilah's eyes. She was beautiful, kind—everything a man wanted in a woman. The better question was—what did she see in *him*? He'd brought her nothing but trouble.

She was also going to be the mother of his child and he wanted her in his life, even if the thought of raising a baby scared the bejesus out of him. Not like he'd had a decent example from his own father.

"Time's up. I've got my answer," she said softly, turning away from him.

"Lilah, wait. You know I—" Great. *Now* he'd found his voice?

She never turned. Her footsteps padded down the hallway and then came the firm click of a closed door.

UNIFORMED COPS AND men in suits swarmed the Elmore County sheriff's office. Harlan stepped through the entrance in time to see J.D. exit his office.

"What the hell is going on here?" he bellowed, one hand reaching in his uniform shirt pocket.

Bet he'd pay a pretty penny for a cigar right about now, Harlan thought.

J.D.'s eyes narrowed as he spotted him in the crowd. "You got something to do with this, Sampson?"

"You bet I did."

Lewis slid him a warning look and he bit the inside of his cheek. They'd discussed this beforehand—he was to let Lewis interrogate J.D. while he tackled Lavon Tedder.

Sammy jumped up from his desk and came over. "What's going on?"

"It's time we cleaned house." Harlan shot a meaningful glance at Alvin who sported a sweat stain under his armpits.

"Could have told me this was coming," Sammy said with the slightest note of reproach.

"Sorry. It was put together late yesterday and I was told to keep it under tight wraps."

"Guess I can understand that. No wonder I was told to bring Lavon in this morning."

"He's already here?"

"Interrogation Room B. We've got his dad in Room A. Tom's on his way with Ed Stovall in tow."

"Thanks, Sammy." Harlan briefly clasped his hand and made his way to Room B, eager for a second crack at Lavon. He'd make the jerk break this time.

Zelda rushed over and handed him a large envelope and file. "I've prepared everything they said you'd need."

He opened the envelope, nodding when he saw its contents. "Perfect."

She scurried back to her desk before he had a chance to study her closely. She'd worked with J.D. for many years. What did she think of all this? He would ask later. For now, he had a job to do.

The interrogation room was as minimalistic as a jail cell, housing only a scarred metal table and a few folding chairs. An aggressively bright fluorescent bulb shone down from the ceiling—the better to spotlight the person being questioned.

Lavon was tilted back in the chair so far his head touched the back wall. He had his arms folded in front of him and his perpetual scowl was in place.

"You again," he complained as Harlan walked in and sat across the table.

"Yep. And this time J.D. and your daddy can't bail you out of trouble."

"I don't believe you."

Harlan glanced at his watch. "I imagine J.D. will be in handcuffs within the next thirty minutes."

A bit of the smug attitude melted off Lavon's face. "Liar."

"Why lie about that? You'll see for yourself soon enough. Who knows—you two might wind up in the same jail cell tonight."

"I ain't done nothing," Lavon muttered.

"I have an eyewitness who says different."

"Your girlfriend?" Lavon scoffed. "As if that won't look rigged in court. Besides, it'll be her word against mine."

"Her word will be loads more credible than those from some asshole who at age twenty-nine has an impressive list of petty crimes that have escalated over the last year."

He opened the folder and began reading aloud. "Vandalism, Class C Assault, Theft of Property in the second degree, criminal mischief—"

"Lilah's nothing but a whore, just like Darla was. All the Tedder women are the same. Look at—"

A buzzer went off in his head, as loud as a referee's whistle in an empty gym. Harlan slammed the file on the table and lunged.

"Hey, man—you can't do that," Lavon sputtered.

Harlan curled his fingers around the scooped neck of Lavon's black T-shirt. The guy's hazel eyes were inches from his own. "Never. Ever. Talk about Lilah that way."

Lavon gave a forced laugh. "Okay. Cool it, dude."

Harlan slowly released his grip and calmed his labored breathing. He was here to crack Lavon, not lose control of himself.

"Fine. Let's get on with it. We have an eyewitness placing you inside my house last night about seven o'clock. What do you have to say about that?"

He shrugged. "I was home. You can ask my parents. I'm sure they'll vouch for me."

"Just so you know—officers are there now checking for fingerprints."

"They won't find anything," he answered, chin lifting with confidence.

"You think you're safe because you wore gloves? Think again. They'll comb the place for stray strands of hair, too. Bet you didn't wear a hairnet."

Lavon licked his lips.

"Let's cut to the chase. Lilah saw you by my desk, and ten minutes later J.D. was at the door with a search warrant. Luckily, she got rid of the drugs you'd planted. You tried to set me up. Tell me why."

"I told you I was home last night. I had nothing to do with this."

"I'll tell you why you did it. You're involved up to your neck in distributing drugs and J.D. is in on the cut. Y'all saw I was getting a little too close to suspecting the truth, so you schemed to get me out of the way."

"You can't prove it."

"Oh, we will." Harlan cocked his thumb toward the door. "Did you get a glimpse of what's happening out there?"

"No. What?"

Harlan rose and opened the door. "Let me take you on a little tour."

He stayed close by Lavon's side as they went down the hallway and into the lobby. Lavon's eyes widened as he caught sight of all the men and his gaze shifted toward J.D.'s office. The door was open and J.D. could be seen wiping his forehead as three men peppered him with questions.

The incredulous drop of Lavon's jaw was a thing of beauty. Harlan guided him back to the interrogation room. As soon as they were both seated, he opened the envelope. Best to do this before the guy asked for a lawyer and clammed up.

He shimmied the half a dozen shell casings from the envelope onto the table. They were all in individual baggies.

Lavon's jaw tightened. "What's this?"

"We found these on Mossy Creek Trail. Where you and another man shot at Lilah."

"They ain't mine. Probably left behind by hunters."

"The only thing being hunted was Lilah," Harlan said, wanting to shake Lavon like a rag doll.

"Wasn't me."

"You're lying. Lilah heard you while she hid in a cave."

"That don't mean nothing. Her word against mine."

Harlan flicked the baggie. "These mean something."

"Them casings could have come from any number of folks."

"Doubtful."

Lavon's eyes narrowed to slits. "Ain't no way you can pin 'em on me."

"Actually we can and we will."

"How's that?"

"We're getting a subpoena to confiscate all your guns. After that, we'll run a ballistics test to see if we have a match."

Lavon blinked but quickly regained his belligerent stance. "Can't narrow it down to just my gun. It's a common model lots of folks 'round here might have for hunting."

Guy was fractionally smarter than Harlan had guessed, but some time alone in the interrogation room might make him sweat.

"I'll be back shortly." Harlan put the casings back in the envelope and went out the door. At the end of the hall, Lewis saw him and approached. "How's it going in there?"

"Not the greatest. He's not budging on his statement about having no knowledge of the drug ring."

"Time to shake him up a bit more." Lewis pulled a small baggie from his pants pocket and handed it to him.

Harlan held it to the light and peered. "A few hair strands?"

Lewis grinned. "They belong to Lavon. We managed to get them today while he was waiting to be questioned."

Harlan nodded. "I know just what to do with them." Quickly, he strode back to Room B and turned on his cell phone's video before slapping the new evidence on the table. "Recognize these?"

Lavon lifted his shoulders and then dropped them, feigning indifference. "Nope."

"Look closer."

Lavon sighed and looked again. "Brown hair. So what."

"The same medium brown as yours and the same swirl pattern. *Your* hair. We'll have the lab results soon enough."

Lavon paled. "I want to talk to my dad."

"He's being questioned."

"Then I want to talk to a—"

"How long have you been involved in this drug ring?" Harlan interrupted. He was about to lose Lavon. "Tell me the truth. Cooperate with us and this will go a lot easier on you and your family."

"My dad has nothing to do with this."

Now he was getting somewhere.

"Surely, you can understand my skepticism. He already had the moonshine operation in place. It would be easy for him—and more profitable—to substitute drugs for liquor. Not only that, but also his risks were minimalized by having the local sheriff on the take."

"But he didn't." Lavon stood, clenching his fists by his sides. "I didn't need to ask him for a thing. I got involved by myself and started making my own money."

His hazel eyes darkened in horror and a hand flew to his mouth. But it was too late: the self-incriminating words had been spoken.

"Wanted to prove you were your own man, huh? Well, junior, you better start naming names. Do that, and the judge will go easier on you. That, and your young age, should go a long way to shortening your prison term."

"Prison? J.D. promised we'd never get caught." Lavon sat back down and held his head in his hands, his shoulders slumped forward. His back shook, but he didn't make a sound.

Lavon didn't look so tough now. He looked like a young scared kid. Harlan nipped sympathy in the bud. That kid had come too close to hurting Lilah on two separate occasions.

"You going to cooperate?"

He removed his hands from his face. "I want a deal," he said in a hard, flat voice. "And a lawyer. I ain't going to prison."

Harlan stood, slipped his cell phone in his pocket and gathered up the files and the evidence. "Oh, but you are. Yeah, you'll get a sentence reduction for naming the others, but make no mistake, jail time is in your future. I'm going to send a couple of detectives in to talk to you now."

In the hall, he answered Lewis's questioning look with a thumbs-up. "He's ready to name the others."

"Great. This will help break J.D. He's pretty close as it is. I have the feeling he's suspected for a long time that he'd eventually get caught." Lewis shook his head. "And to think he was only a few months away from retirement. Stupid."

"And dangerous." The hair on his arms bristled yet again at the thought of how close he and Lilah had come to being framed. "You going to question Alvin Lee as well?"

"Already did. My impression is that he hasn't committed any crime. He's a weak man that J.D. had just started grooming to be his replacement."

"Okay then. Now we need to focus on the murders. Lavon had no reaction to the trophies I put in front of him. I don't think he's involved with the killings."

Lewis nodded. "I've been watching Ed Stovall's interrogation. He's singing about his limited involvement in the moonshine business, but remains adamant he didn't kill his wife. We'll lay photos of all the murder victims, including his former wife, in front of him to see if we get an unusual reaction. I don't believe we will, though."

"What about Thad?"

"Ed told us where the current still is, and where the liquor's being stored. I've got men out now to seize the illegal moonshine. We'll have a good case to prosecute Thad Tedder for the operation. Most likely, Ed will get off with a fine and probation."

Harlan thought of Ed's three sons. "Glad to hear it. Has Thad been shown the victim photos yet?"

Lewis held up a package. "Got some in here. Let's hand it to Marvin Ashton, the GBI officer who's questioning him. We can watch Thad's reaction from the booth."

Harlan took his place inside the booth with several others watching and listening behind the two-way mirror.

Thad sat across from the officer in the interrogation room that looked identical to the other. And that wasn't all that was alike. Thad's brown curly hair was a touch disheveled, like his son's, and he wore the same smug arrogant look his son either emulated or came by naturally through his daddy's DNA.

"Like I keep telling you, I ain't done nothing wrong and I ain't talking to nobody but the sheriff," Thad said.

"And like I told you, Sheriff Bentley's unavailable. You're going to have to deal with me on the charges of distributing illegal liquor."

"I ain't got to do shit."

"It'll go a lot easier on you, and your son, if you cooperate."

"You leave my boy outta this."

"Too late." Marvin smiled with no humor. "Lavon's already confessed."

"What? But he ain't even—he doesn't—"

"Not involved in your business?" Marvin asked. "Maybe not in the moonshine operation, but he's confessed to a much bigger crime. Drug distribution. He's looking at a long prison sentence."

Thad raised his arms and tugged violently at his hair. "No. He wouldn't... I don't believe you."

"They're typing up his confession now. I can show it to you when it's finished, if you'd like."

"Where's J.D.? I want to talk to him."

Harlan shook his head. Thaddeus's first inclination in seeking help was to ask for J.D. and not an attorney.

"J.D.'s got his own troubles this morning. You didn't notice all the cops swarming the place when they brought you in?"

Thad swiped a hand over his face. "This is going to kill Viola." He shuddered and a sob escaped from his throat. "My boy."

Like father, like son, Harlan thought.

"Not only do we have Lavon's confession. We have Ed Stovall's as well. He's told us everything he knows about what you've been running. Agents are out now taking possession of your still and any liquor stored in your holding place."

Thad smashed a fist on the table. "Damn Ed." A crafty look stole into his eyes. "What I mean is—the man's a liar. He's even suspected of killing his wife. Maybe you ought to look at him a little more closely. If Ed knows so damn much, maybe he's the one who runs the whole shebang."

"And then there's another little matter we haven't covered yet." Marvin pulled a stack of old black-and-white photos out of the envelope and slapped it on the table. "Do you remember these women?"

Thad froze for a moment and then a hand jerked

across the table to pick up one of the photos. "What—can I look at these?"

Without waiting for permission, Thad picked up the first photo and held it—a look of almost reverence in his eyes. His Adam's apple twisted in his throat and he swallowed hard.

"Bingo," Harlan whispered. "We've found a killer."

"Yep. Look at that," Lewis said in a low voice. "Even with a cop in the room, he can't help fondling her photo."

"Recognize the woman?" Marvin prodded.

Thad set the photo down with obvious reluctance. "Never seen her before."

"You're lying. C'mon, tell me the truth." Marvin lowered his voice and coaxed Thad as if he were merely a naughty child. "Get it off your chest," he said gently. "You've held a dark secret inside for over two decades. You knew that woman, didn't you? Knew her intimately."

"No. I done told you, I never seen her before."

Martin laid down more photos, spreading them out. "What about your brother Chauncey and your niece Darla?"

Thad jerked his head back, repulsed. "Put them pictures away from me. And I want a lawyer, before I say another word to you or anyone else."

"You're going to need one."

Martin left Thad and stepped into the witness booth. "Sorry guys. He clammed up. What do we do now? Arrest him on the liquor charges?"

"We can after we gather the evidence," Lewis said.

"Damn it," Harlan muttered. "Lilah's no safer today than yesterday. We've gotten nowhere on the murders."

"For now, she's safe. We have an undercover cop doing ride-bys to your house. And we know more than we did coming in," Lewis said. "We have a prime suspect now for the murder cases. We'll bring Thaddeus back in later and book him for running moonshine. Try to shake him out a little more. In the meantime, we'll keep working on J.D. The man knows something about the murders, I'm sure of it."

"That's what I've said all along," Harlan agreed. "J.D. kept insisting that the two recent homicides weren't connected, and then he didn't want me investigating the old murder cases. To top it off, I discovered that our only piece of physical evidence disappeared."

Lewis gestured to the open door. "Ready to try and break him?"

"Absolutely."

Chapter Seventeen

Was she being followed?

Lilah checked the rearview mirror. The black sedan was still behind her, albeit at a comfortable, non-threatening distance. It seemed out of place here—too sleek and pricey for Lavender Mountain. And she was fairly certain it had followed her route for the past couple turns on the county roads.

She gave herself a little shake. Paranoia, much? But to be safe, she'd texted Harlan her destination, as she'd promised to do whenever she left the house. Lilah pulled up to Aunt Vi's place, relieved to note that the sedan drove past the driveway and continued on its way. Lilah got out of the car and glanced at the gray sky that was pregnant with rain. Wind whipped the trees—they were in for a doozy of a summer storm today.

Viola met her at the door, face swollen and puffy. Lilah's heart squeezed. Her aunt seemed to lead an unhappy, fearful kind of life. Today had to be the worst ever, what with the cops picking up her husband and eldest son.

"They've got my Lavon," Aunt Vi sobbed and swiped at her wet cheeks.

Lilah gave her a hug. "I know. I'm so sorry."

Viola clung for a moment and then withdrew, rubbing her hands on her apron. "Come on in the house," she said with great effort. Even in the midst of a family crisis, her aunt's ingrained sense of hospitality peeked through.

Lilah followed her inside. Although it wasn't yet midday, the house was dark and gloomy. The curtains were drawn tight over the windows and the TV set was off. Nothing interrupted the funereal silence. And it was one of the few times Lilah could recall that she'd been here and there was no aroma of a meal being cooked. Aunt Vi almost always had a stew of some sort simmering in the kitchen.

She sat on the sofa and regarded Viola with concern. "I'm glad you called me to come over," she began. "Thought maybe you'd be upset with me after I told Harlan about hearing Lavon that night in the woods."

"I was at first," she said. "Then I had to admit that somehow I'd lost control of my child. When Lavon was young and lost his temper, or did something naughty, I'd hope and pray he'd grow out of it. But he never did. Things only got worse. He kept getting into trouble. And now they suspect he's a—a drug dealer."

The tears spilled again and her body wracked with sobs. Lilah absently placed a hand over her stomach. She couldn't imagine how painful it must be having your child disappoint you in that way.

"I don't know what to say, except that you are a good

mother, a good person. None of this is your fault. Lavon's an adult and he makes his own choices."

Oh, but she did fault Uncle Thad. Lavon was following in his dad's footsteps by breaking the law.

Lilah bit her lip, reconsidering. No, she couldn't entirely blame Thad. After all, her dad had broken the law as well, and look how great her brother, Jimmy, had turned out. He'd been awarded all kind of medals for his military service in the Middle East.

"Have you heard anything this morning from Harlan?" Vi asked, taking a handkerchief out of her apron pocket and twisting it in her lap. "Have they arrested Lavon?"

"I haven't heard a thing. I'll tell you right away if I do."

Vi nodded. "I'm not worried so much about Thad. He always seems to escape trouble. But drugs are a whole lot more serious than moonshine. I imagine Thad isn't too worried for himself."

That's what came from having the local sheriff in your back pocket. But Lilah didn't point that out.

Viola rounded her shoulders, sat up stiffly in the chair and pinned her with bloodshot eyes. "Do you really believe it was Lavon that shot at you?"

"I do." No sense lying.

Viola's lips twisted. "I'm sure he meant it as a warning shot. He wouldn't hurt his own cousin."

Her tone was weak, defeated, as if she couldn't muster the strength to believe her own words.

"I hope his intent wasn't to harm me. But we'll never know."

Viola shook her head, pushing back a shock of gray limp hair that had fallen in her eyes. "He's not capable of murder. Guess you might find it hard to believe and think I'm just a blind, biased mama for saying this, but I know Lavon. He's no murderer."

Lilah's chest seized and a roar sounded in her ears. Did Viola know something about Dad and Darla's murders? "Who said anything about murder?" she asked quietly.

"Come now, child, their deaths are here between us like a living presence. Don't you feel it?"

"Wh-what do you mean?"

"I mean that whoever killed them probably knew them. What's that they always say on them TV crime shows? You want a suspect, look at the immediate family."

"If you have information, come on out and say it."

Viola stood abruptly and walked to a window, peeking out from behind the lace curtain. "If I'm wrong, you're going to think I'm the sorriest wife a husband ever had."

"Uncle Thad?" Lilah stood and the room spun. Her breath quickened. "Did he kill them? Why?"

"I don't know for sure that he's the killer. Says he didn't do it, but...he lies to me. All the time. He has other women." She dropped her hold on the curtain and faced Lilah. "You ever hear that about Thad? He has run around on our marriage for years."

Yeah, she'd heard rumors; it was a small town after all. "The murders," Lilah said, redirecting her aunt. "Why would he kill Dad and Darla?"

"I'm not sure about Darla, but Chauncey had been blackmailing him for the past few months."

"Dad wouldn't do—" Lilah stopped abruptly and thumped her forehead with her palm. "The thirty thousand dollars. Is that how he got it?"

"Thad paid him cash every week. Oh, your dad swore it wasn't blackmail—that he just wanted extra money to leave his children."

"That's not blackmail. Sounds to me like he just asked Uncle Thad for help."

"But he told Thad that he'd been shortchanged over the years in the moonshine business. Said he'd done most of the work and had nothing to show for it. Chauncey demanded Thad pay up."

She'd always suspected as much herself. Thad and his family always seemed to have money while her dad had always been broke. "It's still not blackmail unless Dad threatened Uncle Thad in some way."

"Thad claimed he was afraid Chauncey would turn him in, but it wasn't exactly spelled out."

Lilah bit her tongue. It all sounded pretty nebulous in her opinion. Dad would never have turned in his own brother. Besides, he'd get in trouble himself.

"Thad's been worried that if the cops found out, they'd suspect he had a motive to kill Chauncey. When they took him away this morning… Well, I can't help wondering if the cops are questioning him about that."

"Why are you telling me all this?" Lilah asked slowly. "If the cops don't know, you must realize I have to tell them."

"Yeah, I know." Aunt Viola hung her head.

Lilah mulled over the conversation and Vi's strange behavior. "You suspect Thad's the killer."

Silence hung between them like a ticking bomb.

Vi licked her lips. "It's possible," she whispered.

"You have to tell Harlan."

"Accuse my own husband with no proof?"

Vi stared blankly into space for a few heartbeats. "Always thought his tomfoolery was the worst thing that could ever happen to me," she said flatly. "Then Lavon started getting in trouble, and I thought that was the worst. But that wasn't it neither. For weeks, I've harbored suspicion about my own husband, and that was horrible. But, today…"

Lilah's heart thumped like drum. "What is it?"

"I'll show you."

Vi rose and lumbered down the hallway, her steps as heavy as if her shoulders bore the weight of generations of Tedder sins.

Had her uncle really killed her father? And what about Darla? Maybe the killings were unrelated after all.

Viola returned carrying a leather drawstring pouch. "Found this hid behind the bathroom pipes when I reached for the plunger. I wish to God I never had."

She took the pouch and opened its tie with shaking fingers. Could it be shotgun shells? A confession note? Lilah carefully shook out the contents.

The leather bracelet with its crimson stone, the bright beaded necklace Darla had once worn, the tarnished silver ring with the fake cameo carving and yet another ring with a gold band and small diamond solitaire. Where had she seen that ring before?

"Looks like Darla's wedding ring, don't it?" Aunt Vi asked.

Yes. Of course. At least she could be certain now that Ed hadn't done it.

Her uncle was the Hillside Strangler. And he'd also killed his own brother. Lilah's entire body trembled and she couldn't control the shivering. A bone-deep cold settled in her heart. But past the horror of it all, another question remained. "But why did Uncle Thad kill Darla?" Lilah asked. "Could she have stumbled on the truth somehow and so Thad had to kill her, too?"

Vi made a strangled sound in her throat. "Maybe Thad didn't kill nobody."

"What do you mean? Vi, all this jewelry was taken from murder victims. The fact that you found them here, hidden in your house, means—"

"Could have been Lavon. I'm almost one hundred percent certain it's not, but I can't rule it out neither. And *that*, Lilah, is the worst thing ever for a momma to experience."

"You aren't thinking straight. Lavon's too young to have committed those old murders. It has to be…" She started to say *Uncle* but the word died on her lips. She would never refer to him as that again. "It has to be Thad."

"Maybe Thad killed those women. Could be Lavon killed Darla, and maybe your dad, too," Vi pointed out.

"What reason would Lavon have?" She racked her brain. "Maybe Lavon overheard something and thought my dad was a threat to Thad?"

It still didn't explain Darla, unless Lavon thought

Darla knew something incriminating about Thad or their business.

Lilah hurriedly stuffed the jewelry back in the pouch. It made her skin crawl to think of her sister and the other two women who'd been killed. And almost as sickening, it made her cringe to imagine Thad fondling the pieces of jewelry while reveling in the memory of their death at his hands. "I need to take this to Harlan straight away."

Viola's tears started anew. "I hope I done the right thing."

"You did what any decent person would do," Lilah assured her. "Thank you."

"Maybe you can just tell Harlan you came to visit me and found it on your own? Leave my name out of it?"

"I always tell Harlan the truth," she said gently. "But if he sees fit, maybe he can fudge over this part of how I got the jewelry."

"I don't know what's to become of us all now," Aunt Vi said with a moan.

"Hopefully, we'll all be a little safer," she said drily. Lilah felt sorry for her aunt, but her sympathy only went so far. If Viola had come forward earlier, she might not have been almost killed on two occasions now. She'd been lucky that she and the baby and Harlan had escaped unscathed.

"I've got to go." Lilah rose and dug her car keys out of her purse, eager to get to the sheriff's office. An ironic smile ghosted across her lips. All those officers swarming to get to the bottom of the murders today, and here she was going to walk in there with the physical evidence they needed to actually make a case.

She walked to Vi and patted her shoulder. "Do you want to stay with us a few days? Or I could take you wherever you'd like. Maybe stay with someone until this blows over? I don't want Thad to hurt you."

Vi shook her head. "He don't scare me none. Never has. Not even now."

A car sounded in the driveway, a door opened and shut and then heavy footsteps started up the porch steps. Could Thad be home already? Had to be either him or Lavon.

She glanced at Vi. "Sure you're going to be okay?"

The door flung open with a bang.

"What are you doing here?" Thad asked.

His hair was more disheveled than normal, and his eyes darted back and forth between her and Viola.

"I invited her over," Viola said, lifting her chin a fraction.

"After the way her boyfriend's treated me and our son this morning? Who else is here? Looks like a damn undercover police car's parked in front of the house, too."

He glared at Lilah and she nervously clutched at her purse's shoulder strap. "I'll be going now." She faced Aunt Vi one last time, offering a silent invitation for her to leave as well.

Vi shook her head.

Thad stared at the couch, incredulity written on his face. "What's this?"

He brushed past her and went to the couch.

Sunlight streaming through the open front door cast a spotlight on the diamond solitaire set of Darla's wedding ring. Sparkling prisms of colored light glittered like a beacon, mesmerizing Lilah like a trance.

Thad carefully picked it up and turned to them. "Where are the others?"

The quiet, calm voice frightened her in a way his earlier belligerence had not. She took a step backward.

"Stop," he commanded in that same smooth low tone. "Not another step."

"Leave her alone," Aunt Vi said. "It's over."

He didn't spare his wife a glance. "Where's the rest?"

Lilah spun toward the door and he was beside her in a flash, painfully gripping her forearm.

"Give me my things," he said with a hiss.

"Okay, okay." With her free hand, she dug the pouch out of her purse.

Thad let go of her arm and snatched it up. His body was tense, his focus on the pouch all-absorbing.

Run now.

Lilah scrambled across the den to the back door. A strong pull on her purse ripped into her shoulder and she started tumbling forward. She clutched at the wall with one hand and righted herself.

"Thad, stop it!" Aunt Viola threw herself between Lilah and Thad. She glanced back at Lilah. "Go!"

She didn't need to be told twice.

Chapter Eighteen

"You lost her?" Harlan yelled into the office phone. "How the hell did you manage that? Never mind, I don't want to hear your excuses. When did you last see her and how long ago?"

He checked his cell phone. Lilah had texted him thirty minutes ago she was going to visit her aunt. He should have insisted they hold Thad until Lilah had returned home. So much for trusting another person to keep an eye on her. If anything happened to Lilah, it was on him.

"Is there a problem?" Sammy asked.

"Yeah those agents that were tailing Lilah called. Apparently, she's gone missing. I've got to go."

Sammy grabbed his cruiser keys. "I'll drive. Where to?"

"Thaddeus Tedder's."

They hightailed it to the cruiser. Thunder rumbled in the distance and already a few fat drops started falling. Sammy put on the blue light through town. Once they hit the main county road, he shut it off. "Fill me in on what happened."

"All I know is that Lilah texted me that her aunt had

called and wanted her to visit. Lewis assigned an under-cover cop to tail Lilah, so I thought all would be fine. But the guy called and said that Thad had returned home and he heard screaming from inside the house. He knocked on the door to investigate, and was told that Lilah had run out the back door and into the woods."

Sammy frowned. "Here we go again. But if the cop's with Thad, she should be safe."

Harlan held on to that thought for the ten minutes it took to arrive at Thad's. He strode up the porch and marched inside, not bothering with a knock.

Thad was sprawled on the sofa, head in his hands, while his wife sat at the far opposite end, as if trying to keep the farthest distance possible. The undercover cop sat across the room. He rose and nodded. "Brian Forney, Georgia Bureau of Investigation."

Harlan dismissed him with a quick nod.

"I'll take a look around out back," Sammy offered, standing in the doorway. "See if Lilah's hiding close by."

"Thanks."

Lilah knew Sammy. If she was near, she'd go to him. Harlan faced Thad. "What happened?" he demanded.

"It's time to do the right thing," Viola said. "Lilah knows the truth and so do I. Might go easier on you if you tell it."

Harlan pinned him with a stare. "Spill it. I need to find Lilah."

"It was me," Thad said, staring down at his feet. He drew a loud, unsteady breath. "I killed them hookers."

"Their names were Raylene Rucker and Amzie Billbray," Harlan corrected. "They had names and friends and families."

Forney spoke up. "After all these years, we've captured the Hillside Strangler."

We? The man hadn't done anything except lose Lilah and plop his ass in a chair. But whatever.

"What did you say to Lilah?" Harland continued, focusing on Thad. "Officer Forney heard shouting."

Thad reluctantly lifted his head. "She had my things. I lost my temper."

Harlan's own temper threatened to snap. "Did you—"

"Nah, I didn't lay a hand on her. Vi came between us and made me listen to reason. Lilah ran out the back door—she was scared."

Forney unlocked a pair of handcuffs from his belt and started toward Thad. "I'll handcuff Tedder and take him in."

"I'm not done talking to him yet," Harlan snapped. The officer was champing at the bit to take Thad in and claim he'd had a hand in capturing the murderer. Not that it mattered to him, but he wasn't finished with Thaddeus.

"You confess to killing Raylene and Amzie. What about Chauncey and Darla? Did you kill them as well?"

"Nope. I didn't do it." Thad picked up a leather pouch in his lap and cradled it in one palm. "I couldn't kill my own kin. Takes a special kind of sick to do that."

As if there was much of a distinction. As if Thaddeus had a moral imperative higher than any other murderer. Those kinds of hypocritical rationales were the sort spouted by hard-core inmates from inside a state penitentiary.

"Save it for the judge," Harlan barked. He needed to break Thad now while his wife was encouraging him, and before he got locked up in the county jail and had time to worry about saving his ass from the death penalty.

Yet every second that ticked by, he was aware that Lilah was alone and frightened in the woods. He hoped any moment that she and Sammy would walk through the door.

Viola sniffled and spoke up. "What's going on with Lavon? Is he coming home tonight?"

Poor woman. She was fixin' to have a lifetime of lonely nights in an empty house. "No. He's confessed to distributing drugs and has been charged."

"He'll be locked up for years," Forney added.

Harlan shot him a warning look. That comment wasn't necessary and did nothing but waste valuable time. "Perhaps you can visit him tomorrow," Harlan said to a sobbing Viola. He turned his attention back to Thaddeus. "What's that in your hands?" Harlan asked.

A spark of nearby lightning lit the room, followed closely by a clap of thunder. Sheets of rain assaulted the walls and windows. Damn it, Lilah was out in this storm.

Thad didn't respond to the storm or the question.

Viola jumped up, her thin body trembling. "Give that damn thing to the cops," she screamed at Thad in a high, shrill wail. "What the hell kind of monster did I marry?"

She snatched the pouch out of Thad's hands. No doubt, the man would have put up a fight if he hadn't been so startled by his wife's uncharacteristic outburst.

Viola thrust it at Harlan. "He's ruined my life and Lavon's life. Our boy thinks the world of his daddy. Wanted to be just like him. But at least Lavon's not a killer."

Harlan opened the pouch. It was all there. All the missing evidence. "How did you get the bracelet back? J.D. give it to you?"

Thad nodded.

The depths of J.D.'s despicable behavior stunned Harlan. He'd suspected his boss of turning a blind eye on the drugs and marijuana trade—but murder? That was a whole new level of low.

Harlan picked up the diamond ring and held it to the light. "Darla's?"

"Yeah, but I didn't kill her. I swear!"

"Then how did you get possession of her wedding ring?"

Thad clamped his mouth shut.

"These are all related," Harlan insisted. "Lilah found the jewelry taken from the strangled women in her dad's cabin. Chauncey was killed. She gave the necklace to Darla, and then Darla was killed. Lilah wore the bracelet for a time—now someone's after Lilah."

"You want to serve time for all the murders?" Forney cut in. "Maybe we can cut a deal for the old murders, but not for two members of your own family."

Damn Forney. The last thing Harlan wanted was for Thad to start thinking about arranging deals. He wanted the name of the second killer. And he wanted it now.

To hell with protocol. Harlan grabbed a fistful of Thaddeus's shirt and hauled him to his feet.

"Who is it?"

LILAH TORE THROUGH the backyard and into the woods without a backward glance. It was like the earlier chase—except this time she knew the face of the killer. And instead of heading down the mountain, this time she'd be fleeing upward.

"Lilah! Get back here!" Thad's voice boomed from behind.

Fat chance.

The familiar pine-strewn path was narrower than she remembered from her childhood days. The needles were slick with rain and mud slushed her sneakers. Her feet sank into the ground that had instantly turned to a sticky, sludgy mess. It slowed her progress and strained her calves, but the good news was that it would be much more difficult for her heavyset uncle to sludge his way through the muck.

She was going to make it—unless he returned to his house and got his gun. She was fit and fast, but she couldn't outrun a bullet.

No, no. Aunt Viola would stop him. *Focus on one step at a time*. That was the way to get through this.

Low-lying branches slapped at her face, chest and arms. Her T-shirt and jeans clung to her body and her teeth chattered. Her right shoe stuck in the mud and she stopped to grab it. Leaning against an oak, she slipped it back on and paused to catch her breath. Not too much farther to go to reach safety.

A burst of thunder roared and she cringed. The danger of getting hit by lightning might be better than the chance of Thad lumbering nearby. Rain continued pouring and she sighed. Time to get moving again.

She crossed a small wooden bridge over a swollen creek and knew she was close. Squinting through the downpour, Lilah spotted the cabin and the welcoming warmth of light from a window. She sprinted to the porch and peered through the foggy glass pane.

Uncle Jasper was seated on the sofa with the family bible open in his lap. A shotgun hung over the fireplace mantel. Here she'd be safe and protected.

It was surprising that he hadn't heard her clumsy stumble onto the porch, but the storm must have drowned out the noise. He enjoyed solitude and met visitors on the porch, usually not inviting them into his inner sanctum.

Lilah rapped at the window. She must be a sight—as wet and as muddy as a stray dog left to fend for itself in the harsh elements.

Jasper dropped the bible and half rose from the sofa, squinting his eyes at her form. Bedraggled as she must have appeared, she was recognizable and the startled consternation in his gray eyes morphed to one of surprise.

He disappeared from view a moment and then the back door screeched open.

"Lilah? What are you doin' out there in the rain? Everything all right?"

"I—I think so."

She wanted nothing more than to throw her arms around her uncle's quarrelsome old neck, but he would have hated that. Lilah took a quick glance over her shoulder. Past Jasper's junky backyard, the tree line to the woods loomed large and foreboding, as though it contained ancient dark secrets and harbored beasts both animal and human.

But no Thad emerged, wielding a gun.

Jasper waved her toward the door. "C'mon in."

She hugged her elbows at the waist and entered as Jasper shut the door from behind.

"I was running from Thad. I was afraid he'd hurt me."

Jasper tugged at his beard, regarding her calmly. "I tried to warn you. He's a dangerous man."

"I didn't know how dangerous. Not until Aunt Vi handed me the jewelry she found. Did you know —"

Jasper walked to the window and drew the curtain closed.

"Did you see him? Is he out there?" she asked breathlessly.

"It's just the two of us."

Her shoulders drooped in relief and she sank down onto the sofa. The cushions were still warm from Jasper's body. Her uncle settled in the rocker across from her.

"He's a murderer, Uncle Jasper. The Hilltop Strangler. He killed those two women and…and I think he might have killed Dad and Darla."

His brows rose. "That so?" he asked, as though she'd commented on the weather.

"You don't believe me?" She waved a hand dismissively. "It's true. There's proof. We've got to call Harlan. Tell him to arrest Thad."

"You haven't already called?"

"No. I left their house without my purse or anything.

He wanted to kill me, Uncle Jasper. It was in his eyes. I ran out the back door and Aunt Vi got between us. I ran straight here."

"So you did." He picked up his pipe from the side table, filled it with a pinch of tobacco and proceeded to light it.

"Don't you get it?" she asked, frustrated by his wall of calm. "I was chased through the woods. Thad could be here any moment."

"Not likely. He's too lazy for that."

She shook her head, disappointed and hurt at his lack of concern. She would take care of this herself. "Where's your phone?"

"Ain't working." He drew on the pipe and then exhaled cherry-scented smoke. "Storm must have knocked out the line."

Damn it. Lilah buried her head in her hands and fought against the urge to scream in frustration. Instead, she jumped up. Action was the antidote to get through this ordeal. "We've got to lock the windows and doors."

Luckily, there were only three windows. She latched the front door and eyed the shotgun. "That thing loaded?"

"Always is."

"Good."

She eyed him as he rocked in the chair, puffing away. "Can you close the back window while I get these up front?"

"You ain't got nothing to fear from Thaddeus now."

"You don't understand. Aunt Vi found jewelry he stole from those women he murdered. He'd hidden it behind the bathroom plumbing. He walked in on us and saw that we knew. It made him crazy. He wasn't going to let me take the evidence to Harlan."

"Course not. This is most unfortunate."

"Unfortunate?" Lilah snorted. "I'd say it's a bit more dire than that. Thanks for your concern," she added bitterly.

"You set everything in motion the minute you came back here to Lavender Mountain and found that stuff Chauncey stole." He made a tsking sound. "A shame Thad couldn't have found it first."

"Are you talking about the money? Why does it matter who found it?"

"I ain't talking about the blackmail money."

"Look, I don't know what trash Thad's filled your head with, but Dad didn't blackmail him," she said hotly. She'd had it with everyone putting down her dad, especially when it came to his own brothers. "He knew he was dying and asked Thad to help him out. For us. His kids."

Her throat swelled, threatened to close shut on her. Okay, so taking the money wasn't her dad's finest moment. But he'd done it for Jimmy and Darla, and for *her*. In his own bumbling way, he had wanted to help.

The scent of cherry tobacco made her stomach roil. It clung heavily in the room now that one of the windows was shut. Which reminded her—Lilah strode past him and slammed the back windows shut, too.

"You mind not smoking right now?" she snapped. "I know it's your house, but it's making me nauseous."

Jasper scowled. "It's never bothered you before." His

eyes traveled down her body. "You ain't with child are you? I've heard rumors."

Lilah bit her lips. She'd deliberately not said anything to Uncle Jasper, knowing his strict religious bent. But since he'd outright asked… "Yes. I'm pregnant."

"Harlot."

Lilah shook her head. He hadn't really said that—had he?

"You turned out no different than those fallen women Thad killed."

Jasper dropped his pipe in the ashtray and it clanged as loud as a dropped shotgun shell. Burnt ash spilled out of it like bits of molten lava. Lilah couldn't tear her gaze away. She didn't want to look up and see the disgust in Jasper's face.

"I thought you were different from your sister," Jasper continued. "She was always trash. But you—I had hopes you'd turn into a decent, respectable lady." Gone was the detached tone and odd indifference. His voice crackled with condemnation. "Now look at you. Pregnant, unwed and living in sin."

She lifted her chin. "Don't you dare talk about my sister that way. Or me, either. After today, you'll never have to see my face again. Trust me on that."

"No doubt."

The eerie calm had returned, as though he'd slipped back on a mask.

"How about letting me borrow your truck," Lilah said stiffly. She wanted out of the smoky, stuffy room. "I'll see it's returned to you tomorrow."

Jasper bent over, picked the bible up from the floor

where he'd dropped it earlier and then rifled his fingers through a jar filled with ink pens. He selected a crimson one and laid it in the middle of the book where their ancestry tree was located.

Crimson.

Ernest, Dad and Darla's names had been scribed in the color of blood.

Lilah took a step backward. "If you'll just give me those truck keys," she said desperately. "I'll go away and never come back. Promise."

"We both know it's too late for that. Poor LayLay. You'll be the hardest one of all."

"I—I don't know what you're talking about." She took another step backward, mind in a whirl. Somehow, she'd stepped into the twilight zone. "Look, just give me the keys—"

"Chauncey was a blackmailer. A man can't treat his family like that. It's wrong."

This was no alternate universe. This was real. If she wanted to survive, for her baby to live, she'd better get it together.

"You're right," she agreed, playing along. "It was wrong. Dad shouldn't have done that."

"I had to kill him. What kind of man threatens to turn his own brother into the police? Chauncey found that jewelry and guessed the truth. Only a matter of time before he ruined everything."

"You knew Thad killed those women?" she asked, breathless.

"From the start."

Jasper stepped past her.

She couldn't help asking. "Why didn't you do something?"

"They were nothing but harlots. An abomination. Still, he shouldn't have killed them. We had an agreement. He wouldn't tell anyone I'd killed Dad, and I'd keep my silence."

He lifted the gun from the mantel and cocked the slide, checking the chamber. "Yep, loaded."

"But killing your father was like—self-defense. Right? He hurt you."

"That's the way I seen it," Jasper agreed. "Shot him cold in the back and claimed it was a hunting accident. Only mistake was that I didn't know Thad was watching."

"So when you found out Thad strangled those women, you couldn't say anything for fear he'd turn you in."

"Exactly."

Lilah backed all the way into the doorway, feeling behind her for the door handle. Where was it?

Jasper gave a crooked smile. "Go on and open the door. We'll take a little walk."

What was she thinking trying to get outside? Better to stay inside. Jasper was crazy—not stupid. If he shot her in the cabin, he would never be able to cover up the crime. "It's—it's raining," she stammered, grasping at straws.

He barked a laugh.

She scooted along the side of the wall, away from the door, not daring to turn her back on Jasper.

"Did you kill Darla, too?"

"Had to. Stupid chit. All over that cheap glass bauble.

Thad and I tried to reason with her, offered to get her another necklace in exchange. But she'd taken a shine to it. Or so she'd claimed. Kept asking why it was so important to us, demanding to know why we wanted it. She always was the sassiest little ole thing."

Lilah hoped that the killing had been quick, that Darla hadn't known what was coming. "So y'all argued. Did you force her to hand over her wedding ring?"

"That came afterward. Thad said the missing ring might make it look like a possible robbery."

No, Thad had only wanted to expand his sick collection of tokens. They were both responsible for her sister's death, but she still wanted to know who had pulled the trigger.

"Was it you or Thad that shot Darla?"

"Me. I'm the eldest. The one who cleans up his little brother's mess. 'Sides, Thad's a coward at heart."

"Big words from a man who shoots defenseless women in the back."

The broad side of his free hand smacked her across the face and she fell to the floor. Pain exploded in her right cheek and ears. Lilah hunched up, instinctively shielding her stomach from another blow.

The next landed on her right thigh—a vicious kick.

"Get up," he commanded.

Lilah scanned the room, desperate for a weapon. Her eyes lit on the bible and she crawled to it, picking it up and clutching it to her chest.

"Put that back on the table," he ordered. "You ain't worthy enough to be holdin' it."

"You wouldn't shoot a woman holding a bible, would

you?" She inched away from him, needing to get out of striking range.

Jasper swooped down and grabbed a handful of her hair. "Get up now!"

The book fell out of her hands and she rose to her feet, tears blinding her eyes. "Okay, okay. Please stop hurting me."

His grip released a fraction. "And now we take that walk."

He marched her to the door and thrust it open. Her scalp was on fire.

This was it. She was going to lose the baby, lose Harlan, lose her life. In ten minutes, she'd be nothing more than another death her uncle recorded in crimson ink.

Wind swept the rain onto the porch and the sky rumbled. He would force her into the woods now and shoot her in the back like he'd done with Dad and Darla.

"Please," she begged. "Don't shoot me. I won't tell anyone."

"Damn straight you won't."

HARLAN CLIMBED IN the cruiser, adrenaline spiking his body like a bolt of lightning. Lilah had run from the lion's den right into the belly of the beast.

Sammy scrambled onto the seat beside him. "I'll radio for backup," he said. "We'll send a search team to check the woods in case she didn't make it all the way to Jasper's."

He didn't answer. All his attention was on the slick roads. The windshield wipers blasted away sheets of rain, squeaking out a message. *Hur-ry, hur-ry, hur-ry.*

"We can't help Lilah if you get us killed on the roads," Sammy warned. "Should have let me drive again."

"I got this."

"She's going to be okay," Sammy promised.

He had to believe that, had to cling to that bit of faith. Otherwise, he couldn't function.

The tires squealed as he rounded a bend a bit too quick. The cruiser spun wildly in a half circle before he regained control.

"Not so fast," Sammy cautioned.

Easy for him to say. His wife and kid weren't in danger.

Finally, *finally* he arrived at Jasper's.

Two figures were on the porch. Damn this rain. His vision was limited to one-second patches of clarity as the wipers continued their frenzied action. He hit the accelerator and then skidded to a halt at the ramshackle cabin.

His heart jackhammered at the sight of Jasper poking a shotgun at Lilah's back. *No!* He jumped out of the car, pulling the pistol out of his side belt.

"Stop!" he ordered. "Drop the gun, Jasper."

Lilah's gray eyes, turbulent as the storm clouds above, lit on him.

And then, he knew the truth.

He loved her.

Madly. Heartbreakingly, bone-crushingly loved her. Probably always had. How could he have been so stupid for so long? He couldn't lose Lilah. Not now—not ever.

"Let her go!" Harlan ordered. "Set the gun down and put your hands in the air."

Jasper lowered the shotgun to his side, but he grabbed Lilah in a chokehold with his free hand.

"You ain't takin' me alive," he shouted. "And if I go, she goes, too."

Jasper backed up to the door. Bastard was planning to barricade himself in the cabin with Lilah as his hostage.

"Don't do it, Jasper," he warned. "Let her go now or it will only end up worse for you."

"Couldn't be no worse," he huffed, dragging Lilah with him.

Lilah pulled at his arm and kicked his shins, but Jasper's hold didn't loosen.

He couldn't let Jasper get her inside the cabin. Harlan holstered his gun, lunged forward and leaped up onto the porch.

Jasper shoved Lilah to the side and started raising his shotgun.

There was no time to draw his pistol, or get out of Jasper's way so Sammy would have a clear shot at the bastard. Harlan did the only thing he could do. He dove at him, hoping to knock the shotgun out of Jasper's hand before the shot went off.

He didn't make it.

A roar exploded and a tremendous pressure burst on his left shoulder. Lilah's scream echoed in his brain. *The shotgun*. He focused his eyes on it and managed to fall forward, knocking it out of Jasper's hand. It clattered on the wet rotting floorboards of the porch.

"Harlan." Lilah leaned over him, eyes wide in horror. He felt blood ooze from his shoulder. Soon, the pain would set in. For now, shock and adrenaline kept his mind sharp and focused.

"I'm okay," he said with a rasp. "Go get in the car and stay low."

Jasper's footsteps pounded by them. Coward was running away.

Harlan pulled himself to a seated position. He could still shoot with his right hand if Jasper came back toward them.

"Halt, or I'll fire!" Sammy yelled, aiming his pistol at the fleeing Jasper.

Chapter Nineteen

Sammy fired a warning shot in the air, but Jasper kept running—drawing closer to the edge of the woods.

Lilah lifted her chin. *Get in the car, my ass.* Jasper was getting away. The man who had killed her dad and her sister and had almost killed her.

She picked up her uncle's fallen shotgun and steadied it against her right shoulder. With no hesitation, she racked the chamber and took aim through the drenching downpour.

Boom.

Jasper's body twitched in the air and then hurtled to the ground.

Got him.

Dead center through the heart, if she wasn't mistaken. Shot in the back the same way he'd murdered his own kin. Justice could be a bitch sometimes—but not today.

"Good job," Harlan drawled, his voice weak.

Lilah set the gun against the wall and knelt beside him, kissing him soundly on the mouth. "Let's get you to the hospital," she said, helping him to his feet.

Sammy rushed over to them and slid his shoulder

under Harlan's right arm. "Lean on me." He tossed Lilah the keys. "Open the back door and start the car."

She caught the keys in the air and turned.

"Hey, Lilah," Sammy called. "Great shot."

"That's my girl," Harlan added.

THE HOSPITAL ROOM was filled with flowers and fruit baskets. A large window on the far wall allowed a view of bright stars glistening over the mountains, as well as a few lights from cabins in the hollows.

Who would have thought a hospital room could be so cozy or so beautiful?

The nurse had finally shooed out the slew of visitors, declaring her patient needed rest. Despite their speedy arrival at the hospital, Harlan had lost a lot of blood. They'd given him a transfusion and were keeping him overnight for observation—much to his disgust.

Lilah lay down on her cot beside the sleeping Harlan, close enough so she could reach out and touch him. He'd claimed not to be tired, but ten minutes after the nurse had run off his guests, the medication had done its job and he'd drifted away. Gently, she ran her fingers over his right hand. She should have been exhausted, but she was wide-awake.

And so damn grateful to be alive and with Harlan.

"Hey, gorgeous," he mumbled. "You're still here. You should go home and rest."

"Hush. I'm exactly where I want to be. With you."

Harlan squeezed her hand and she enjoyed the peaceful silence between them—the sort that is most appreciated after the passing of a storm.

"Can we get it right this time?" Harlan asked, breaking the quiet. "A ring, a wedding—the whole nine yards."

Her mouth curved upward. "You asking me to marry you again?"

"I won't stop until we're properly married," he said. "I know I can be a pompous ass, and my future's uncertain—"

"It's not," she argued, picking up the silver star badge on the end table. "Lewis Slidell left this for you." She pinned it on his thin cotton hospital-issued gown. "You're the new sheriff in town and quite a catch."

He held her arm. "Doesn't mean we have to stay here. I'm willing to leave Lavender Mountain if that's what you want."

Her breath caught. Being the sheriff was his dream job. "You'd do that for me?"

"I'd do anything to have a chance with you again."

"Is that the medication talking?" she asked with an unsteady laugh.

"Hell, you know I love you, Lilah. My life was never the same once you walked in it." He grimaced. "Only took a life-or-death situation to make me realize the truth. Can you stand to be married to such an idiot?"

Which left the original problem that had destroyed their relationship the first time. "What about your career? Won't being hitched to a Tedder destroy your reputation?"

Harlan winced. "Anyone who knows you realizes that I'm the lucky one." He drew a deep breath. "And if we're getting everything out in the open, there's something you should know. It was never about whether you were good enough for me. I'm the one not good enough for *you*."

"You? You're damn near perfect, Harlan," she argued.

"I've told you about my father. I promise you, I'll do everything in the world not to be like him. I want to be the kind of husband and dad that you and the baby deserve. Here or wherever you want to live."

Damn, she loved this man. And, truth be told, she loved her home. Together, they would raise their children nestled in the same ancient mountains where they and their families had lived. Harlan would make it a safer place; she had absolute faith in him.

She leaned over the hospital cot, kissed him chastely on the forehead and started to pull away. Harlan tugged her with his uninjured arm and she fell on top of him. "Harlan!" She giggled. "We can't. What if the nurse comes back?"

He gave an exaggerated sigh. "Guess I'll have to wait until we get home."

Home with Harlan— that had a nice ring. "Just a few more hours. And then we'll have the rest of our lives together."

* * * * *